THE PRINCESS AND THE SEAL

THE PRINCESS AND THE SEAL

A NAVY SEAL ROYAL ROMANCE

ALANA ALBERTSON

BOLERO BOOKS

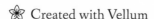

AUTHOR'S NOTE

To instantly get a free full length book, Deadly Sins, sign up for my newsletter: **Free Book**

DEDICATION

*To every girl who has ever kissed a frogman and prayed
he would turn into a prince.*

THE PRINCESS AND THE SEAL

"She's a princess, and I'm a frogman. If I kiss her, I'll turn into a prince."

A love affair. One week in France.

She's a classy princess; I'm a low-down and dirty SEAL.

She's been promised to another man; I'm married to my Team.

She plans to commit to a loveless marriage for her country; I'm willing to die for mine.

Until I fall in love with her.

Nothing will stop me from making her my woman. Centuries ago, I would have defeated my enemies in battle, claimed her as my prize, and been crowned a king. Who says I can't turn back the hands of time? I'm a Navy SEAL—the ultimate warrior. No one will stop me from getting what I want.

And I want this princess.

EPIGRAPH

THE FROG PRINCE

When the princess awoke on the following morning she was astonished to see, instead of the frog, a handsome prince, gazing on her with the most beautiful eyes she had ever seen and standing at the head of her bed.

He told her that he had been enchanted by a spiteful fairy, who had changed him into a frog; and that he had been fated so to abide till some princess should take him out of the spring, and let him eat from her plate, and sleep upon her bed for three nights.

'You,' said the prince, 'have broken his cruel charm, and now I have nothing to wish for but

that you should go with me into my father's kingdom, where I will marry you, and love you as long as you live.'

— THE BROTHERS GRIMM

CHAPTER 1

RYAN

I DOWNED MY SHOT OF WHISKEY in a single gulp, the smooth liquid coating my throat and relaxing my mind as the train rolled into Bayeux, France. Gazing out the window, I had to catch my breath due to the beauty of the picturesque landscape: towering trees, a bright blue lake, and old stone dwellings completely mesmerized me. It was definitely an upgrade from where I'd spent my last seven months. My skin still felt singed from the scorching heat of the desert hell where I had been fighting ISIS.

I grabbed my pack, stopping for a moment to stare at the camouflage nylon duffel bag containing my belongings. A memory popped into my head—me as a young boy, clutching my teddy bear and a black plastic trash bag as I lugged my few possessions to my next foster home, praying that my new caretakers would welcome me into their family and make me their son forever.

Spoiler alert—they didn't.

Twenty years later, I was still alone, a warrior with no place to call home.

That was the way I liked it.

I stepped into the station, a faceless man among throngs of people. I admired the last glimpses of the sunset over the city steeples with a massive mountain looming in the background. A river flowed through the center of town. Pine trees, spicy herbs, and fragrant flowers scented the air. Vacation had begun.

Though I'd deployed overseas many times, I'd never been to Europe. I'd only been in France a few hours, but I was worlds away from my hometown in Gilroy, California.

I would check into my bed-and-breakfast and spend a day relaxing in town before renting a car and heading to Omaha Beach.

For the next week, I would live my life selfishly. I planned to visit all the historical battle sites I'd dreamed of seeing as a kid, even when everyone told me I'd never make anything out of myself, never leave my piss-poor town.

I'm here now, a complete badass.

I had one week to recuperate from the hardships of war by fucking some hot European chicks, who preferably wouldn't even speak English so I could smash and dash.

Time to get started—I was ready to sample the local cuisine, and then I needed to find a woman.

I studied the map on my phone, and I plotted my route to a place to eat and then to the bed-and-breakfast.

As I put my phone in my back pocket, my gaze quickly focused on a beautiful blonde sitting on a stone bench, her nose buried in a book. Maybe she'd tuck me in and give me a nightcap.

Admiring her curves, I zeroed in on my target before noticing two swarthy men hovering in her shadow.

Why were they standing so close to her?

Before I could approach, one snatched her purse,

knocking her to the ground, and ran off to the left. The other grabbed her luggage and came straight at me.

"Au secours!" she screamed. *"On vient de me voler!"*

I leaped into action, tossing my pack aside and tackling the motherfucker.

He scrambled to his feet and swung wildly. I ducked out of the way. With a firm kick to his ribs and a punch square in the face, I knocked him out.

I knelt down beside him and slapped him on his sallow cheeks until he came to. His brown eyes blinked open, then locked on me with a watery gaze.

A small crowd had gathered, but none of the bystanders stepped in to help. "Where's your friend?"

He shook his head.

I rolled him over onto his stomach, pulled a cell phone out of his back pocket, and frisked him for weapons. I found a switchblade, pocketed it, and then flipped him back over like a pancake. "Call him and get him to bring back her purse."

"No English."

Liar. The chances of recovering this woman's purse

were fading by the minute. I was sure the thief had stolen her money and credit cards and tossed the purse into the river.

I grabbed the guy by his throat and forced myself not to choke him out. The last thing I wanted was to get arrested overseas for assault. I'd have a hell of a time explaining that to my CO, my commanding officer. Instead, I pulled him up by his clothes, retrieved the lady's luggage, picked up my pack, and marched him over to the woman. I'd let the police deal with him.

I scanned the distance for the other thief, but there was no trace of him.

A few people were staring at me, but I didn't give a fuck. The blonde still cowered on the ground, and not a single passerby had approached her to see if she was okay.

I threw the thief back on the ground and tied his wrists to the bench post with one of my shoelaces. "Don't try anything funny, or I'll kill you."

He didn't respond.

I turned my attention to the beautiful woman, reached out my hand, and helped her up.

She stood gracefully then smoothed her hands over her clothes and looked right at me. Long, thick eyelashes framed her large eyes, which hypnotized me with their unusual cornflower-blue shade. "*Merci beaucoup, monsieur.*"

I eye-fucked her slowly. She looked like she was in her early twenties, and her golden-blonde hair framed a stunning heart-shaped face before it cascaded down to her ample cleavage. Heat pulsed through my veins—she was a knockout. "I don't speak French."

Her face brightened. "You are an American?" she asked in perfect English laced with a sexy accent.

I gave her a charming smile. "Damn straight."

America was the only woman I'd ever loved. I'd bleed for her; I'd die for her.

"I can walk you to the nearest police station to file a report. Or we can call the cops. Do they have nine-one-one over here?"

She shook her head no, and her lower lip trembled. "That won't be necessary. I doubt the police would be able to recover my purse. Please, just let him go."

Confusion set in. "You don't want to call the police? Why let this bastard get away with his crime?"

"I just don't want the trouble, okay? It's hard to explain. Please . . . let him go."

I exhaled. I didn't want to let this jerk off the hook, but it wasn't up to me if she didn't want to press charges. Why did she want to keep this quiet? Maybe she was on the run from someone or something.

Whatever.

I reluctantly released him. "Piece of shit. Get the fuck out of here."

The man broke through the crowd and scurried away like a scared little mouse.

What kind of motherfucker stole from a gorgeous woman? He was lucky I hadn't killed him, but I'd killed too many men in my life. There was no room for death on my vacation.

I handed her the luggage.

"Thank you for retrieving my suitcase. How can I ever repay you?"

By getting on all fours and letting me fuck you from behind.

I pushed the thought away. Over the years, I'd grown very good at reading people, and my gut told me she wasn't the type of woman who would be interested in a casual hookup. Besides her designer luggage, she wore a loose silk blouse that looked like it was expensive and sported huge emerald earrings.

And a massive diamond engagement ring.

Dammit. I was looking for a one-night stand—not someone else's relationship drama.

I had two rules when it came to women: never sleep with the same one twice, and never fuck some other man's woman. Cheaters repulsed me, especially after seeing so many of my Teammates return home from deployment to find their wives had been unfaithful.

"No need. Are you hurt?"

She placed her hand on my arm.

"No, I'm fine. A bit rattled, but I'll be okay." She gave me a brave smile that faded after a few seconds. "Other than the fact that my documents, my money, and my phone are gone."

That sucked. "Can I escort you somewhere? Your hotel?" I'd take her somewhere she would be safe. I didn't owe her anything else. She was engaged—I refused to get involved.

Her shoulders dropped, and her voice sounded weak. "I don't want to be a bother."

"You aren't a bother. I'm happy to help."

"I appreciate that, but I'll be fine. Thank you again for getting my luggage." She grabbed her bag from me, walked a few feet away, slumped on a bench, and clutched her book. I watched curiously to see what she would do.

After a few moments, she began to cry.

Fuck. I couldn't leave her alone after she had just been mugged. I wasn't *that* much of a dick.

Fine, Ryan. Just get her situated and then go on your way.

I walked to the bench and sat beside her. "What are you going to do? I have a cell with international minutes. Would you like to call someone? Maybe your fiancé?"

She bit her plump lower lip and fidgeted with the

diamond on her finger. "Oh, you noticed my ring. It's not what it seems."

I rolled my eyes. "Sure it isn't, lady. Tell that to him."

"I mean, it is. I'm technically engaged, but we're not together romantically. It's more of . . . a business arrangement."

I leaned in closer. What was her story? I didn't know her at all, but something in her voice and her eyes made me curious about her. Normally, I didn't give two shits about other people's personal lives, but she intrigued me. I had to get to the bottom of this.

"An arrangement? That's sexy." What year was it? Who still had arranged marriages?

She sniffled and gave me a pointed look. "It's not meant to be sexy. It's meant to be practical."

I wasn't even going to go there with her. I was of the firm belief that the words *marriage* and *practical* should never be used in the same sentence.

"Where are you staying?"

"At the Château La Chenevière. But without my documents, I'll be unable to check in. I could call my father, but I'm too embarrassed. He warned me about traveling alone. He'll just tell me, 'I told you so,' and I'll never hear the end of it."

Daddy's girl. An engaged daddy's girl. Even so, she spoke with an innocence I found refreshing. "I get it. You want to be independent."

She looked up at me. "It's not just that. Now I realize he was right. It was foolish of me to travel alone. This is none of your concern—I'm sorry for taking up so much of your time. Don't worry about me. I'll be fine."

But she didn't look fine. She forced a smile like she was trying to keep everything together and not break down.

I studied this woman next to me who didn't seem to blend in with either the casual locals or the sloppy tourists. Even though I was on vacation, I was a Navy SEAL twenty-four hours a day, seven days a week, fifty-two weeks a year. I wouldn't be able to forgive myself if something happened to her. She'd already been mugged, and though I'd recovered her luggage, she didn't have her purse. So far, she'd been sweet, shy, and was surprisingly open to answering all my questions. Nothing like the other women I'd hooked up with. Definitely a challenge.

And I never backed down from a challenge.

"Let me take you to dinner first, and after we're done, I'll walk you to your hotel and make sure you're settled."

Her brow furrowed. "I'm not sure that's a good idea. I don't want to ruin your night with my troubles. Furthermore, I don't even know you."

I needed to assure her that I wasn't some psychopath. I scooted away from her. "Then get to know me. My name is Ryan Shelton, I'm a Navy SEAL." I reached into my back pocket and flashed a military ID at her.

Her eyes widened. "A Navy SEAL? I read once that Navy SEALs were trained to kill in over three hundred ways. So, you're a killer? That's supposed to make me feel more comfortable with you?"

Not the reaction I was going for and definitely not the one I was used to. Back in the States, many women dropped to their knees with mouths opened in anticipation when I told them I was a SEAL.

I put the ID back in my pocket. "I protect people, just like I protected you earlier. I'm one of the good guys. What's your name?"

"Giselle. Nice to meet you, Ryan."

"Would you like to join me for dinner or not?"

She played with a lock of her hair and stared at me. After an uncomfortable pause, she finally said, "I'd love to."

"Great. Let's go." I took her luggage and walked down the street with her right beside me, her heels clicking on the cobblestones. I took a moment to stare at her luscious ass, which sent a jolt to my cock.

As we walked further, I kept stealing glances at her, trying to assess her. Giselle had perfect posture, luxury clothing, expensive jewelry, and an elegant way of speaking. I still couldn't place her accent—I wanted to say it was French or Italian. Still, judging by her grammar, it was obvious that she had been educated in English-speaking schools.

Maybe she was the daughter of a diplomat. Or of a global entrepreneur. Or of some head of a cartel or Mafia-type organization. Or from a deeply religious family. Who else would force her into an arranged marriage?

I'll find out tonight.

After walking only a few minutes, a man darted in front of us, his camera flashing in our faces.

"Gisela! Votre Majesté!" He was speaking so rapidly that I couldn't follow what he was saying.

What the fuck? I knocked the camera out of his hand, but it was attached to a strap around his neck. The man yelled more words I didn't understand and continued taking pictures of us.

Giselle shielded her face and ran up the street. The man chased after her.

Where was she going? Who *was* this girl?

I bolted after her, racing past the loser with the camera, tripping him on the way.

Once I reached her side, I grabbed her arm then turned her to face me. "Why is a paparazzo taking pictures of you? Who are you? Don't lie to me."

Her eyes blinked like she was deciding whether or not to tell me the truth. Finally, she spoke.

"I didn't lie to you. My name is Giselle . . . Garabaldi."

She looked at me expectantly, as if the name should mean something.

"I'm afraid I'm not current with Swedish pop music." I took a stab in the dark.

She gave a bitter, mirthless laugh. "No. I'm not a singer."

"I'm lost, babe. Are you famous or something?"

"Yes, you could say that. I'm the Crown Princess of Santa Cariña."

CHAPTER 2

GISELLE

"*Y*OU'RE A FUCKING PRINCESS? Are you kidding me?"

"Yes, indeed, I am. Could you please lower your voice? And I would appreciate it if you would refrain from swearing at me. I find it very jarring."

His eyes widened. "I'll talk however I want. This is my vacation, and I'm not one of your subjects." He scratched a hand along his full dark beard, highlighted by the silvery moon. "You're royalty, and you're traveling without protection? Not a good idea, Princess."

He obviously had a point. My father had warned me against going alone, insisting I travel with security, but for once in my sheltered life, I'd stood up to him. I told him that if I was old enough to get married, I was old enough to travel alone. But he'd been right. Clearly, I had been unable to take care of myself. Just the thought of calling the palace to tell my father I'd been mugged was worse than being cursed at by this foul-mouthed stranger.

Make that an incredibly sexy foulmouthed stranger. Ryan was the complete opposite of my blue-blooded fiancé.

He typed something on his phone. I leaned over; he was staring at my official photo. Ugh, I hated that photo. It was so airbrushed that I looked like I was made out of plastic.

His eyes flicked between his phone and my face.

"Yup, that's you. Wow, I thought you were lying."

"I never lie." To other people, that was. I only lied to myself.

I could see his eyes reading over my Wikipedia page. I cringed—my public relations team made me sound like a perfect, prim prude of a princess. Mentioning that I was the spokesperson of True Love Waits, which promotes abstinence until marriage, didn't exactly scream sexy. I closed my eyes and prayed that he hadn't read that, and if he did, he wouldn't know what it meant. I might as well have had the word *virgin* tattooed on my forehead.

I stammered, at a loss to explain myself.

What should I say?

As if he could sense my uneasiness, he put his hand on my shoulder. "I'm impressed." He then bowed dramatically in front of me. "Let's go, Your Royal Highness. Your royal escort awaits."

Great, now he would treat me differently. For once, I'd wanted to be seen as just a normal girl. I hadn't planned to tell him I was a princess until after dinner, hoping he would get to know me first. But that photographer had forced my confession.

We arrived at a bistro with a red awning and neon lights. A chalkboard outside listed the specials, and the scent of rosemary, thyme, and bay leaves made me salivate.

"Is this place nice enough for you, Princess?"

I was used to restaurants with three Michelin stars, but I never enjoyed them. The food was excellent without a doubt, but I always found the atmosphere pretentious.

"It's lovely."

Ryan spoke to the maître d'. "Table for two."

The man attempted to store our luggage, but Ryan stopped him and asked if we could keep the bags near us. I almost laughed and accused Ryan of being paranoid—I seriously doubted the maître d' would steal anything, but clearly, Ryan was overly cautious. The maître d' agreed reluctantly and then seated us at a table in the back of the restaurant. The lights were dim, and I was grateful that the bistro had very few customers.

I felt a flutter in my stomach. What if someone recognized me? But the other patrons didn't even seem to glance at us, so I studied the menu and tried to relax.

Now that I could see Ryan better, I was taken aback by how handsome he was. His brown hair was longer than I figured men in the military would have, and his soulfully deep brown eyes were accented by long black eyelashes.

Ryan ordered a bottle of Bordeaux. I quickly glanced

at the wine list—he had chosen the most expensive bottle in the restaurant.

Was he trying to impress me? My skin heated up—was it hot in here, or was I just a nervous wreck? This was starting to feel like I was on a blind date.

Was this a date?

"You really don't have to do this. I can pay you back tomorrow."

He shot me an intense glare. "I got this. I don't need your money. I've never been out to dinner with a princess. Let's just have a good time tonight."

He relaxed those broad shoulders back into the chair, his gaze lighter than before. "So, tell me, why are you traveling alone? Must need a break from all your tough work of attending balls and kissing frogs."

What a jerk. I bit my lip. "I'm taking a solo trip before I have to get married. And for your information, I do full-time charity work. I help ill children, refugees, and the elderly. It's immensely gratifying. I'm truly blessed."

He cocked his head. "You're a regular Princess Di. That's cool. Where's your fiancé? How would he feel if he knew you were on a romantic date with a dangerous man like me?"

Romantic date? Dangerous man? Excitement swirled with fear low in my belly. What were his intentions toward me? How was tonight going to end?

I hadn't missed how he'd paused over the word "dangerous." But I didn't fear being with him because he'd beaten up my mugger. Maybe my blind trust was foolish, but I hated to admit that I was more scared of being alone tonight than of being with this handsome stranger.

"He would be displeased. Not because he cares about me, but because it would make him look bad. Honestly, I don't know him very well. We've only met a few times. We've never even kissed." I quickly covered my mouth and winced. Why had I just admitted that?

Ryan shook his head as if in disbelief. "Wow. Some love story."

Explaining my engagement out loud made me realize just how truly ridiculous my predicament was. Why couldn't I just stand up to my father and say no?

"It's embarrassing. I don't even know where he is at

the moment, though I've heard he is out—how do you Americans say it—sowing his royal oats . . . before the wedding." And that was true. The tabloids had picture after picture of my betrothed partying with every socialite in town.

Meanwhile, I was portrayed as a pathetic, lovelorn princess. At first, I'd hoped we would someday grow to love each other as my parents had before my mom's tragic death. But my royal wedding would be nothing like their love story—mine would be more like a funeral. A funeral for my psyche.

Ryan's eyes traveled over me from head to toe. "What a douche. Why would he want to be with anyone else when he has you? If you were my woman, I wouldn't let you out of my sight."

Warmth spread through me like wildfire. His compliments came off as sincere, like they weren't just rehearsed lines. What would it be like to be this self-proclaimed dangerous man's woman?

Sadly, I would never find out.

I attempted to change the subject.

"What about you? Tell me about your family."

He gazed over my head. "There's nothing to tell."

"There is always something to tell. What state are you from? Do you have any brothers or sisters? What do your parents do?"

I detected a hint of sadness in his eyes but was probably overanalyzing the situation.

Before he answered me, the waiter came to take our order. Ryan chose the beef daube, and I requested the salmon with lentils.

I looked at him expectantly, but he ignored my earlier questions about his family and took a sip of wine. "Why are you marrying him? This isn't the fourteen hundreds. Prince Arthur married his college sweetheart Elizabeth by choice."

Why did everyone always bring up Art? As young royals, Arthur and I had practically grown up together, though these days, I spent more time with his younger brother, Prince Douglas. "Arthur is the future King of England. He can do what he wants. I'm the princess of a very tiny principality. Our income is mostly from tourism. We don't even have our own military. We rely on other countries for support, defense, and trade."

He let out a loud laugh.

I scowled at him. "Something funny, Ryan?"

"No wonder you travel without security. That's sad that you don't even have your own military, but not shocking."

Breathe, Giselle, breathe. Calm, cool, collected.

"Is that so? As I said, we are very small. What would you suggest, Mr. Navy SEAL?"

He licked his lips. "Hire me. I could fix the military problem."

Now it was my turn to laugh. "You could, could you? You could fund thousands of people to form an army, go to war with France to emancipate us, and provide aid to a town that is virtually landlocked by the entirety of Europe?" Who did he think he was? God? "The truth is, we love our neighboring countries. But that doesn't mean we can stop being strategic."

"And the strategy is to marry some random guy?"

"Hardly random. Our parents arranged us as children. My fiancé's name is Miguel. He's from Quintana, a small country near Spain. He's been pleasant enough the handful of times we have interacted, but I don't know him well."

Ryan's eyes widened. "You're actually going to marry some guy you barely know? I love my country—hell, I'd die for her—but I wouldn't commit myself to a love-less marriage. What if he's horrible in bed?"

Of course he went there. I scowled at him. "Is that all you men think about? Sex? There's more to a marriage than intercourse."

He grinned and then gave me a wink. A wink that slayed me. Mischievous, sexual, dangerous. He reached his hand across the table and took mine. "Trust me, baby. Sex is the most important aspect of a marriage. It's the glue that binds you together and makes your relationship different from your relation-ship with everyone else in the world. My buddies love their wives so much, they would do anything to get back to them. Their sexual connection is the reason they last through long separations. Without that chem-ical attraction, that lust, that hunger, you have nothing."

His words hit me like a bolt to my chest. What if he was right? What if I was repulsed when Miguel touched me? Or what if Miguel didn't enjoy sleeping with me? What then? Would I just wait at home while he found pleasure with other women, knowing full well we would never be granted a divorce?

I pushed that image out of my head. "Then why aren't you married?"

"Because that life's not for me. I don't want to be tied down to anyone. I want to be free to come and go as I please. All I care about is being a SEAL. Nothing else matters."

"Well, that's depressing. At least I'm giving love a chance. Your life sounds lonelier than mine."

He bared his teeth at me but didn't speak, instead downing his glass of wine like it was a shot of whiskey.

Gotcha. This bad boy Navy SEAL was just as messed up as I was.

The waiter brought our meals, and we ate together in tense silence.

This was ridiculous. What had I been thinking when I'd agreed to go to dinner with this man? Our worlds couldn't be more different.

Despite the awkwardness, we shared a delicious dessert of figs, pralines, and ice cream. When the bill came, Ryan quickly paid, I thanked him, and we exited the restaurant.

We walked a few blocks, the moonlight guiding our steps. For a second, I pretended this wasn't a pity date, and we on our honeymoon, newlyweds who were madly in love. What would that be like? To marry someone I was truly crazy about, someone who couldn't keep his hands off me?

I would never know.

The wine had relaxed me, and I forced myself to live in the moment. I turned to him under the stars. "Thank you for dinner."

"It was my pleasure. I find you fascinating."

My heart raced. "How so?"

"You lead an interesting life. You're nothing like the women I've met before."

I was pretty sure that was a compliment, but he had been so hot and cold with me that I had to make sure. "Oh, really? How am I different, other than the 'I'm a princess' thing?"

He brushed a stray lock of hair back off my face. "You're beautiful, classy, and sweet."

Woozy from his words, I pulled back from him. I had to end this night before I did something I would regret.

"That's very kind of you to say. I had a great time as well. You are very . . . dynamic. You really didn't have to wine and dine me. I'm sorry I put you in the middle of this situation."

He took my hand, and heat filled my core. "Don't apologize. I could stare at you all night."

He pulled me to him. His wine-spiked breath blew hot on my neck, and my pulse quickened.

What was he doing? Was he going to kiss me?

My legs wobbled. Our faces were so close. There was a burn mark on the side of his neck, possibly from a cigarette. Who had left that mark on him? When? Was it during a battle? Somewhere else? Had he been tortured?

He'd said my life was interesting, but what type of life had this handsome stranger lived? I wanted to know everything about his past, but for now . . . all I wanted was to be kissed by this man.

Just when I didn't think I could stand the tension of

being this close to him for another second, his hand cupped my face, and his lips took mine.

His mouth was rough, not soft like those of the boys I'd fantasized about in my youth. His other hand traveled farther down my back, landing on my bottom as adrenaline coursed through my body. I pressed my palm against his chest, feeling his hard pecs, imagining seeing him with his shirt off.

Was he trying to seduce me? Did I want him to?

All I knew was that I wanted this kiss to last forever.

But seconds later, he pulled away, a sly look on his face.

I caught my breath. "What was that for?"

He laughed. "You're a princess. I'm a frogman. I thought if I kissed you, I'd turn into a prince."

CHAPTER 3

RYAN

*H*ER DELICATE AND MANICURED hand swiftly smacked my jaw. "So much for that theory, Ryan. You will never be a prince. You're still just a vulgar SEAL."

My face stung after she slapped me, but it was okay—I deserved it. Hell, I enjoyed it. Damn, if she had that fire in the bedroom . . . A bolt of electricity shot straight to my cock. I imagined tying up this princess, talking dirty to her, and fucking her hard until she could do nothing but come and come for me.

But before I could seduce her, I needed to get her to agree to stay with me. Yes, I wanted her, but I also wanted her to feel safe.

Her sweet taste lingered on my tongue. I meant everything I'd said to her earlier. I couldn't stop staring at her angelic face and banging body. Giselle was a bombshell. She was unlike any girl I'd ever met. Well, that was the understatement of the year. She was a fucking princess.

My princess.

The princess and the SEAL. I liked the sound of that.

I had spent every day of the past seven months looking forward to this vacation. Dreams of sex, sins, and sunsets had filled my fantasies. I had wanted nothing more than a string of hedonistic indulgences with any women who caught my fancy. And when it was over, I'd planned to return home and go back to my normal, familiar life. *Alone.*

But after one date with Giselle, I wanted something a little different.

I wanted to spend my entire trip with this princess.

I embraced the challenge she presented. I'd seduce her, make her fall for me, and leave her with the lasting memory of how important sexual chemistry was. Then maybe someday she'd find the courage to leave her loser fiancé for a fulfilling life with a man who truly loved her. A man who wanted to be a husband and a father and was suitable for stuffy royal life.

A better man than me.

She might even find me one day and thank me.

Time to tell her.

"Change of plans, babe. You're staying with me tonight."

A look of horror registered on her face. "What? No. I would never."

I knew that look of fear; I'd seen it on my enemies many times right before taking their lives. But I wasn't used to seeing it on a woman.

The last time I saw that look was on my foster sister's face. *That night.*

I closed my eyes and forced away my past. *Never go back.* I was now a man, a skilled warrior, and no one could hurt me. *I will never be that scared, helpless little boy again.*

I pulled myself back to the present and looked at

Giselle. She was fidgeting. I didn't want to make her uncomfortable.

Fuck. I had come on too strong. I needed to dial it back. She was nothing like the women I usually met; she was clearly sheltered. I couldn't blame her for being afraid. She knew nothing about me, and I had to admit I'd been giving her a hard time since I met her.

Be a gentleman. It was hard to model a behavior I never saw growing up, but I'd give it a try. For Princess Giselle.

I took her hand and kissed it, relieved when she didn't pull away. "I'm sorry. I didn't mean to scare you. Let me try again. I think it's in your best interest to stay with me tonight."

She eyed me suspiciously. "You do, do you? Does every girl you meet just hop into bed with you?"

Yes, actually, but she didn't need the details.

I dropped my smug smile. "I'm not trying to seduce you, Giselle," I lied. "You're a princess, and you have the paparazzi stalking you. Have you already forgotten that you were mugged today? You don't have any ID or money. You're not safe. I'll be your bodyguard tonight until you get your affairs in order if you let me."

Peach blossomed across her cheeks. "That's a very kind offer, Ryan. I do appreciate it, but I don't think it's a good idea. I'm engaged, as I said, so it wouldn't be appropriate."

Right, the lame playboy fiancé who didn't even want to fuck this beautiful woman was cockblocking me. What was wrong with him? It would be one thing if he was gay, then I'd get it, but she herself said that he was sowing his wild oats. What a dick. It didn't make sense.

"You said he was hooking up with people. Why would he care if you spent the night with me?"

She threw up her hands in disgust. "Because I'm a lady. I'm sure you are aware there is a double standard about what is acceptable for men and women in the public eye, especially royalty. But it's not even about that or him. He's not the reason I can't stay with you."

I would never, ever understand women. I shouldn't even bother trying. "Then what's the reason?"

She cast a downward glance, and her voice lowered to a whisper. "You will laugh at me."

I took her hand. "I promise I won't laugh. Just tell me."

"Fine." She let out an audible exhale. "I've never stayed overnight with any man." She shrugged her shoulders and looked down again. "Or even been alone with one. I usually have a chaperone, but I didn't let her come with me on this trip."

Laughing wasn't even an option as my jaw dropped in full shock and disbelief.

Was she for real? Had *never* been alone with a man?

"How old are you?"

"Twenty-two. And a half. You?"

"Twenty-seven." I lifted her chin to stare into her eyes. She didn't look away. "Babe, are you telling me you're a virgin?"

Her cheeks flushed. "Not that it's any of your business at all, but yes, I am. It is what is expected of me. Actually, I think it's quite romantic, saving myself for marriage. It will make my wedding night special. I've only ever wanted to sleep with one man—my husband. Give myself completely to him and him alone. Forever."

What the—?

My stone-cold heart skipped a beat.

A virgin? A princess? *A virgin princess?* Had I won the lottery? Was this really happening to me?

How was this even possible? I'd never met any woman in her twenties who was still a virgin.

But Giselle was royalty. Standard rules didn't apply.

Maybe I was on some type of hidden camera show. Or maybe this was some sort of cruel joke my buddies had set up to prank me. Tonight was too good to be true.

But I knew there were no cameras around; I had already scanned my surroundings. And my buddies were way too wrapped up enjoying their own lives to pull off something like this, especially in a foreign country with a real-life princess.

Maybe this was just my lucky day.

And this night was getting better and better.

Virgins usually held no appeal for me. I'd always been drawn to sexually confident and free women—women whom I could fuck and forget. The responsibility of taking a girl's virginity would weigh too heavily on my conscience. At least that was what I'd always assumed up until now.

But I'd never been with a virgin, and the more I

thought about it, the more I liked the idea. An inno-cent girl whom I could teach. A girl who I knew had only been touched by me was surprisingly attractive.

My cock became rock hard in anticipation.

I would be her first lover. She would remember me forever.

What would it be like to be the first man to suck on her nipples? Be the first man to lick her pussy, fuck her, make her come for me and only me?

I'm going to find out.

Time to lay out my cards. There was no holding back; I was all in.

"Sweetheart, I'm not going to touch you unless you want me to. I'm not that kind of guy. I won't take advantage of you."

And I meant it. If she didn't want me, I'd back the hell off.

If.

"Why should I trust you? You've probably been with hundreds of women."

I wasn't going to lie. "My past doesn't matter. I live my

life by a code—I serve with honor and integrity on and off the battlefield. If I have to, I'll stand watch outside your room, so you feel comfortable. I don't need to sleep—during Hell Week, I only slept four hours in a total of five days."

"Really? That's insane."

"Yeah, it was. But worth it. I survived and became a SEAL. And now I know I can do anything I put my mind to. Right now, that's protecting you. I'm not walking away until I know you're safe. I'll never forgive myself if something happens to you."

Her eyes widened, and she softened toward me. She rubbed my shoulder, her fingernails tracing my muscles.

Yup, I was in.

"Wow. You would really do that for me? Why?"

I nodded. "Yes, I would. It's my duty to protect you because tonight you have no one else to do it. Look, I'm booked into a bed-and-breakfast a block away. I'm sure your château is some fancy five-star hotel, but that's not how I roll. I don't feel comfortable having you stay somewhere else alone until I know you'll be traveling with someone who can protect you. You'll be safe with me, safer than you will be by yourself. So, what's it going to be?"

She swallowed hard. *Those lips could suck on my cock, swallow down* . . . Damn, I couldn't wait. I'd been deployed for seven months and hadn't been with a woman since before I went to Iraq. Just sleeping in the same room with a beautiful woman would be a welcome change from camping next to my Teammates, even if she made me stay on the floor.

"Okay, but only because it's late, and I don't want to call and wake my father."

Score. "Good choice." That was easier than I'd thought it would be.

A small part of me knew I hadn't invited her to stay with me just because I wanted to seduce her; I truly wanted to make sure she was safe. But now that she'd agreed, I was going to have some fun.

I put my arm around her shoulders. "Come on, Princess, let's go check in." I looked around the cobblestone street. "Do you think there's a market open?"

She tilted her head. "Why? Do you need something?"

"Just peas. I'm going to place some under the mattress to verify your identity."

She laughed. "You're quite the comedian, Ryan. What I want to know is if you're going to slay any dragons for me?"

I pulled her into my arms, her scent intoxicating. "I've slain men far more dangerous than dragons, sweetheart." And I had. "I'll do anything for you."

I kissed her again, probing her fiery mouth with my tongue, drunk on her sweetness.

Her soft lips welcomed me, and I was lost in her. She pulled away, and my heart raced. I couldn't wait to get her alone and see how far she'd go with me, but I would not force myself on her. I wouldn't touch her if she didn't want me.

But judging by the way she'd just kissed me, I was confident that she already did.

I grabbed our luggage, and we walked toward the bed-and-breakfast.

The thought crossed my mind that a few centuries ago if I'd met a princess, I would've just kidnapped her, claimed her as mine, killed my enemies in battle, and been crowned king.

Ah, the good old days.

Who said I couldn't turn back the hands of time? I was a SEAL, the ultimate warrior. No one would stop me from getting what I wanted.

And I wanted this princess.

CHAPTER 4

GISELLE

 Y LIPS BURNED HOT. HIS mouth, his tongue, his heat. I had never in my life known that a kiss could ignite me like this.

But the cool breeze dampened the flame.

As we walked down the street, the desire to flee threatened to overtake me entirely. My heart pounded, and sweat beaded on my forehead. What if Ryan was a serial killer? Or a rapist? How utterly naïve was I? Even though he had tackled the man who'd mugged me, and shown me his military ID, that didn't mean he was a good man.

But when I was with him, I didn't worry about my

safety. As stupid as that sounded, I would rather be with him than be alone at the château. And the thought of checking in now without any documents and money was dreadful. I did not want to call my father and have him say he told me so.

It was only for one night.

Ryan had correctly guessed that I'd been booked into a five-star hotel. I'd considered arguing with him, insisting on having him stay there with me, but then gossip would start about me spending the night with a handsome stranger. That was definitely publicity I didn't need. Though I didn't love my fiancé, I had no desire to disgrace him, my father, or my country. The press would never let me hear the end of it.

He easily found the entrance to the bed-and-breakfast as if he had stayed here before. La Maison Chantal was on the outskirts of town. Before we went inside, he took my hand in his. A jolt surged through my body at the stark contrast of his rough, tanned skin against my delicate, pale hand.

"Do you need to wear a disguise? Or I can give you some cash, you can check in alone, and I can sneak up to your bedroom later." He playfully tugged on my hair. "You're a princess—I could climb up your hair."

"Charming. No, I should be fine, since this bed-and-breakfast is tucked away. I'll just use my best American accent. If we tell the owners we're married, I doubt they will question it."

He stroked my arm. "Married? I haven't even fucked you yet."

The hair on my arm prickled my skin. The way he said *yet* riled me, as if sleeping with him was inevitable, which it most certainly was not. His voice was so deep and dirty, raw, and masculine. So unlike that of the men I'd been around my entire life. "Nor will you ever, sir. You can introduce me as Audrey."

He didn't seem to get my *Roman Holiday* reference. He'd probably never seen or heard of that movie, my personal favorite.

I'd be lying if I didn't admit that I may have even prayed to meet some handsome stranger and travel uninhibited on my final trip as a single woman. One memory of a passionate affair to last me through what would most likely be a loveless marriage. But in my fantasies, the object of my affection had been a cultured gentleman, well read and worldly, not a crass Navy SEAL with an incredible body, dirty mouth, and a filthy mind.

He led me inside the white doors. The walls were made out of brick, and a gold chandelier hung low from the ceiling, almost hitting Ryan's head. A vase of fresh-cut flowers was perched on an entry table, and there was a crackling blaze in the hearth. A small sitting area was filled with books. It was as if I was walking into an old family friend's home. I adored this charming place on sight.

An older silver-haired lady wearing a white scarf greeted us. "*Bonjour.*"

Ryan briefly smiled, revealing his deep dimples. "Hi. My wife and I have a reservation. Mr. and Mrs. Shelton." He squeezed me in his arms in a complete embrace, our chests flush together. I could feel his heart beating strongly. I resisted the voice in my head that told me to pull away, especially since he smelled incredible. Not of expensive cologne and aged cognac, no. Woodsy, earthy. Like he had just chopped wood in a forest and bathed in a babbling brook.

Naked. What would he look like naked? I forced that image out of my head.

"*Bienvenue à Bayeux.* Is this your honeymoon?"

Ryan's hands dropped from my shoulders and gripped

my waist possessively while I forced a smile, my body melting from his touch. "Sure is. I can't wait to get her alone."

I stepped on his foot, but he didn't even flinch.

Ugh, I was doomed.

"Oh, we love newlyweds." She handed us a large metal key, and we followed her up the stairs where she showed us to our room. "I'll be sure to give you love-birds plenty of privacy. Breakfast is served every morning at nine, or I can prepare a tray for your room. And there is a computer in the lobby with free internet."

Ryan moved our luggage into the room and then thanked her, and she left.

Before I could say a word, Ryan lifted me up and carried me over the threshold.

Like a bride.

I laughed. Would my fiancé even be able to pick me up?

Ryan placed me on the bed, and I looked around the room. It was small but cozy, with a tiny fireplace and a large bay window. Soft mauve wallpaper adorned the walls, and a queen-size bed made of cherry wood stood in the center.

A quick scan revealed there was no sofa for me to sleep on. Would he keep his promise to sleep on the floor? Or would we share the bed?

He shut the door and gave me that cocky smirk I was starting to look forward to seeing. *Damn him.*

"That was lovely. You didn't have to put on a show for her sake, though. You could've just said we were married."

Ryan let out a laugh. He flopped down onto the bed and relaxed next to me, and I couldn't help studying his chiseled body. A black T-shirt clung to his massive chest, and I had to look away from the tight denim fabric covering his crotch. I'd never been alone with a man who was not related to me, not even my fiancé. Nerves made me involuntarily shiver.

His gaze burned into me, and I could feel his eyes staring at my chest. "I still can't believe you thought it was a good idea to travel alone. Not too smart, Princess. You know there are terrorists everywhere working on blowing places up."

I shook my head. "You Americans are always so paranoid. I believe in enjoying my life and not living in fear."

That sounded good in theory . . .

But what would it be like if I was left alone? If I had no one?

If I was stuck in a loveless marriage?

"A fucking princess. What a trip. I've never met a princess, though I've met the president's daughter."

I didn't know whether or not to believe him, but since I was stuck in this room with this stranger, I decided to give him the benefit of the doubt. "Well, then we do have something in common. I've met Ava as well. She's a cool girl." I felt a twinge of jealousy. Ava was both beautiful and accomplished. Had he kissed her too?

I shook my head. None of my business.

I decided to change the subject. "So, why are you traveling alone?"

"Because I've been stuck in hell with a platoon of sixteen men for the last seven months. I need some downtime. Alone."

I couldn't even fathom what being at war was like. I wanted to ask him questions, but it would be rude. He'd already admitted to me that he'd killed men—he probably didn't want to talk about it. A big part of being a princess was knowing when to be diplomatic. I changed the subject, hoping to gain some insight into Ryan's personality. "What made you choose Bayeux?"

"I wanted to see the Normandy beaches."

That was surprising. Most Americans would choose to visit my country and watch the drag races or head into Paris to see the Eiffel Tower. "Are you a history buff?"

"War history."

"Interesting choice. It seems to me that if you spent all your life engaged in combat, you wouldn't want to spend your free time visiting battle sites. But you will love Normandy. I'd be happy to give you a tour."

The second those words left my lips, my belly knotted with regret. How foolish I must've sounded—agreeing to stay in this man's room, offering to travel to Normandy with him. I was acting like a desperate teenager.

Of course he wouldn't want some pathetic virgin princess hanging around him on his European adventure. I'd heard about these American men traveling alone in my country. Sleeping with a different girl every night, partying at the clubs, getting drunk. What a wild life.

What would it be like to live my life on my own terms? Indulge in my fantasies of freedom without fearing any repercussions?

He moved closer to me. "I'd like that."

Oh, God—he really wanted to?

No, I couldn't. This arrangement was only for one night. After tomorrow, it would be best for both of us if we never saw each other again.

I needed a good night's sleep. Hopefully, I would behave more appropriately and be able to think more rationally tomorrow.

"I'm sure you're tired from traveling all day. We should get some rest."

"Yeah, I'm beat. I'm going to take a shower."

A shower? He would be naked with only a thin wall separating us. The water spraying his incredible chest. Maybe he would leave the door open, and I could steal a peek.

I tried not to think about how much I was dying to know what he looked like naked.

I had to get out of this room before I did something ridiculous.

"Okay, I'll just wait in the lobby until you are done. There's a library downstairs; I'll choose a book and read by the fire."

He grabbed my wrist. "No, you won't. You're a princess. Don't you realize you could get kidnapped and held for ransom? I'm not letting you out of this room until you get copies of your identification, some money, and I return you safely to your hotel. And you should travel with protection."

I was regretting my decision to stay with him. He was treating me like a helpless child. Just like my father did. "Are you offering your services, Mr. SEAL? Who do you think you are, anyway? My father? I'll be fine downstairs. I'm an adult."

"An adult who was mugged. Not to mention, you're gorgeous. You'll stand out too much. I don't know who else is in this place. End of discussion."

Did he really think I was gorgeous? Over the years, I'd almost come to believe all the nasty tabloid comments about me. Princesses should be lithe, elegant, flawless. I was none of those things.

He grabbed some clothes and a little black bag out of his pack, then winked at me. "I'll only be a few minutes. Don't move, unless," he leaned close and whispered in my ear, "you want to join me."

Yes, I do!

"I most certainly do not."

He grinned and then went into the bathroom and shut the door. The pipes rattled as the water turned on, and I imagined him getting in, his naked body glistening under the water.

I couldn't wait to tell my cousin Lucia about this night. Lucia was a wild one. If she knew I was in a room with a hot Navy SEAL, she'd be horribly disappointed if I didn't hook up with him.

But that wasn't going to happen. Ever.

I glanced down at the phone in the room. I should call my father just in case he contacted the hotel after not being able to reach me on my cell. Ugh, I didn't want to alarm him. But if I didn't call him to check in, he would be even more worried.

What to do, what to do . . .

The water was still running, so I decided to make a break for it. I grabbed the key, snuck out of the room, raced down the stairs, and found the computer desk. I logged in to my email and sent a quick message to my father.

Papa,

I have arrived safely in Bayeux but have unfortunately lost my phone. Luckily, I ran into an old friend from university, and she graciously allowed me to stay with her at a bed-and-breakfast in town. Could you please overnight copies of my identification and my credit cards to my hotel? I'll pick them up tomorrow. Please don't worry about me—I'm safe. I'll call you tomorrow.

Love,

Giselle

Sent.

Ugh, I hated to lie to him, but if I told him the truth, he would freak out. Tomorrow, when I said goodbye to Ryan, I would go to my hotel and call my father.

And try to forget this night ever happened.

I ran back up the stairs, and luckily for me, Ryan was still in the bathroom.

A few minutes later, he emerged.

My mouth gaped.

Good Lord, he was hot. His huge chest tapered down to a narrow waist above the visible line of his boxers, peeking out of his pajama pants. The scent of cologne filled the air.

He gave a slight smirk and asked, "Would you be more comfortable if I put on a shirt?"

I shook my head no, unable to speak, afraid the only thing that would come out of my mouth would be drool.

"Good. Normally I sleep naked, but since you're a virgin and all, I didn't want to scare you."

"How considerate of you." I tried not to stare at all the tattoos covering his broad chest.

"Your turn, *Princess.*"

The way he said "Princess" sounded illicit. Usually, I hated the term, but from those lips, it evoked a sense of sex.

I slowly removed my jewelry and placed it in the top drawer of the nightstand, next to a copy of the Bible. Guilt consumed me as if the good book could tell how much I wanted to sin. I quickly shut the drawer.

I grabbed my nightgown and toiletries from my luggage and locked myself in the bathroom. As I jumped in the shower, and the water hit my bare body, I kept reminding myself that only a few minutes ago, Ryan had been naked right where I stood now. Had he fantasized about me while he was in here?

What would it be like to lose my virginity to this warrior?

I couldn't help wondering if this night was the beginning of a love affair. An affair to remember.

A love to forget.

CHAPTER 5

RYAN

*A*S I WAITED FOR HER IN THE bedroom, I couldn't stop picturing what she would look like naked. Imagining how she would taste. How her body would react to my touch. How incredibly tight she must be.

I needed to be inside her.

But I had to go slow with this girl, so slow it would hurt. I didn't want to make her uncomfortable. I wasn't that guy.

She had to want me. She had to beg me to fuck her, to take her virginity, or I wouldn't touch her.

I had to force myself to not think about ravaging her, so I grabbed a book from my pack. Reading had been my refuge since I was little, much to the shock of everyone who just saw me as some dumb foster kid born to a drug-addicted mom always looking for her next fix. A woman who didn't have the faintest clue which one of the men she'd screwed was her baby daddy.

My mom had lost her parental rights long ago. She didn't even know I was a SEAL. And I was certain that I would never learn the identity of my biological dad. I'd even registered on one of those genetic sites and still had no leads.

Books took me away from my life. Over the years, my tastes changed from books about sharks to war novels. The first time I read *The Red Badge of Courage*, I knew I wanted to join the military. Then, after one of my many foster dads beat me to within an inch of my life, I vowed never to be helpless again. I'd become a Navy SEAL—the biggest, baddest motherfucker on this Earth. No one would ever hurt me or anyone I loved again.

Giselle emerged from the bathroom wearing a silky white nightgown. Damn, she looked incredible. I'd never seen a body like hers. Her breasts were full but not fake, her waist was tiny, and she had extremely curvy hips. Voluptuous, real, a bombshell.

I was dying to see her naked.

Her shoulders dropped, and she covered her chest with her hands when she caught me ogling her. "Sorry, I realize this nightgown is a bit inappropriate. The other ones I brought are of a similar style. I'm not trying to tempt you." Her tone was serious and not in the least bit flirty.

I couldn't wait to touch and explore her body. "Consider me tempted. But don't worry, sweetheart, I have self-control."

"Thank you. I appreciate that." She flashed me a dazzling smile, then looked at my book. "What are you reading?"

"Nothing." I tossed my book aside, wanting to focus completely on her. "Come here." I motioned her over to me. "What's your plan for your vacation?"

She sat on the edge of the bed. "I didn't have anything concrete. See the Bayeux tapestry, visit some museums, travel around this part of the country. Just live life."

"And your fiancé didn't offer to go with you so you could get to know each other? If you were my woman, I wouldn't leave you alone for a minute."

She bit her lower lip. "No, he didn't. I'm not sure that he's fond of me. We're very different. He's more of a playboy prince. Instead of helping his country, he spends his days on his yacht sunbathing, and his nights in the clubs partying."

Her description made me hate him even more. "Sounds like a loser. I can't stand rich motherfuckers who don't work. Especially royalty."

She wrinkled her face. "We aren't all lazy."

"Didn't say you were. He should join the military like Prince Arthur and Prince Douglas. I like Prince Doug —man, that guy seems cool as shit. He held the Invincible Games for wounded vets. One of my buddies competed. Dude is blind, but he's now a Paralympian swimmer."

"Oh, that's amazing. What an inspiration your friend is. Yes, everyone loves Doug. He's a good man. We're quite close, actually."

"Really? I'd love to meet him one day."

"That could be arranged. I'm going hunting with him and Art next year. Maybe I can get you an invitation."

I stared at her. This woman was going hunting with the future King of England? And she just invited me— some American bastard? My own family wanted nothing to do with me, and now I was hanging out with royals.

Look at me now, Mom.

"That would be awesome."

She smiled and looked me in the eyes. "So, what is it like being a Navy SEAL? It must be terribly exciting."

"I love it. It's not just a job, it's my life. My calling. My Teammates are the best men in the world."

"Have you always wanted to be a SEAL?"

"Yup." I left it at that. I did not want to tell this girl about my past, have her pity me, and realize that no one had ever loved me. I had no desire to be emotionally intimate with her or anyone else. Ever. Giselle and I couldn't be more different. She had a royal lineage that could be traced back centuries; I didn't even know who my fucking father was.

I'd spent my deployment planning every aspect of this

trip, fantasizing about backpacking solo through Europe. The rest of my Teammates had returned home to their hot wives, adorable kids, and loving families.

Every homecoming at the port, I rushed past the sexy women holding Welcome Home signs, dodged the newborns waiting to be held for the first time by their daddies, avoided the parents who were so grateful to greet their sons, and beelined straight for the solace of my truck.

My brothers-in-arms invited me into their homes and encouraged me to learn to trust and love someone. But deep in my heart, I knew that my destiny was to be the best SEAL I could be. My buddies with families hesitated before they walked into the line of fire, worried about the loved ones they would leave behind if they died.

I didn't have that problem.

As a SEAL, I never wavered. I was first to fight, last to leave, and always ready to deploy or attack the enemy at a moment's notice.

Need a volunteer to take down a terrorist? I was the man.

I knew that one day, I would die honorably in battle.

And no one but my Teammates would miss me.

It was better that way.

Her eyes widened as she stared at my bare chest. "I've never seen so many tattoos. Did they hurt? Do they mean anything?"

"No, they didn't hurt. Well, not that I remember. I was blazed when I got them. This is a skeleton frog holding a trident, representing my buddy who died last year. And this one is my class number from SEAL training."

"I'm sorry about your friend." She leaned in to get a closer look, but her feet remained planted on the floor.

"Babe, come here. I won't bite. You're safe with me. There's only one bed in here, but I can sleep on the floor if it makes you more comfortable." I meant every word I said to her. I just hoped she believed me.

"I'm sorry. You must think I'm so silly."

I took her hand and interlaced her fingers with mine. "No, I think you're beautiful. And innocent. It's refreshing. I like you."

She sat next to me, and her finger traced along my

ALANA ALBERTSON

tattoos across my chest. Her delicate hand felt
different to me than the touches I'd had from other
women. Giselle seemed enchanted by me, something I
had never really experienced.

She'd claimed not only to be a virgin, but that she had
never been alone with a man. Her sheltered life was
the exact opposite of my hedonistic youth.

But even though she was innocent, her situation was
very complicated. I needed to ask more questions.
"When's your wedding?"

Her face fell. "Next month. When I return from this
trip, we will start the festivities."

When I was a little boy, I envied people like her,
people who were rich and cultured. I'd always
assumed that if only I had been born with a silver
spoon in my mouth, my life would've been easy. But
now I realized her world came with pressures I
couldn't even begin to understand.

At least I was free to be with whomever I wanted.

And I wanted her.

"What would happen if you didn't go through
with it?"

64

Her face contorted as if that was the weirdest question anyone had ever asked her. "I'd be exiled from my country. It would humiliate my father, in addition to my fiancé and his country. The trade agreements between my country and his would fall apart. The military support we have would be threatened. I'd be the laughingstock of the royal world. And these days, with the internet, I'd probably be made fun of worldwide."

Got it. But I didn't want to stop challenging her on this. She needed to think about the outcome of this decision. "So, what you're saying is that you could still walk away."

She huffed. "Ryan, you're impossible. I'm getting married next month, no matter what. I've given my word to my fiancé and my father, and I will honor it."

I was impressed by her commitment to her country. The princess and the frogman had something in common after all. I was willing to die for my country. She was willing to sacrifice her happiness for hers.

I brushed a lock of golden hair back from her face. "I respect that. I'm sure you'll be happy. And don't worry, Princess. Your husband will find you just as beautiful and sexy as I do."

"I'm not sure. He has never even kissed me. We went on a date, and he didn't even try. At the time, I told myself it was because of my chaperone but now I see the truth." She looked so sad.

I shook my head. "Like I said, he's a fool."

I pulled her in for a kiss. She didn't resist; she reclined beside me, her lips welcoming mine. Her hot little tongue traced my mouth, and I couldn't help but think what that tongue would feel like on my cock. I imagined her eyes looking up at me as I fucked her mouth.

Dammit.

Breathe, Ryan.

Her hand touched my shoulder, making its way down to my chest.

Normally, I didn't spend too much time kissing, too eager to fuck and forget. But I wanted to move slowly with her, make her feel comfortable with me.

Her mouth opened wider, and she kissed me deeper, her hands exploring my body. Her nails scratched my chest lightly, and a pleasurable shiver rippled through me.

Then she grazed my crotch, and I was dying to feel her hand on my cock.

I touched her breasts, but she pulled away from me.

"We really shouldn't be doing this. This is very reckless of me. I don't want to lead you on. I plan to remain a virgin until my wedding night. Tomorrow, I'll be out of your hair, and you'll be free to find a woman who will be more than happy to have sex with you, no strings attached. I wish I were her, but sadly, I am not."

I kissed her neck; she tasted like a perfectly ripe peach. "You're not leading me on. I'm enjoying every minute we have together. Let's just enjoy tonight. When you tell me to stop, I will."

CHAPTER 6

GISELLE

*M*Y BODY WAS ON FIRE. I LET MY desire control my mind. "I don't want you to stop yet."

God, I should stop. I have a fiancé . . .

But he's not exactly waiting for me back home.

Two wrongs didn't make a right—but this was beyond right. It was heaven.

Ryan offered me an amused smile. "Good. Now, where were we?" He pressed his body to mine, and I felt every inch of him. I'd never been kissed like this, by a man who clearly knew what he was doing. Yet he didn't seem to be in a rush, nor trying to go further. His kisses varied in intensity. Some were strong and passionate. Others were sweet and playful. But all of them flooded my body with desire.

My nerves tingled, and I knew I was in big trouble.

I explored his chest and caressed his biceps, so hard and huge. I was high on his scent, his sex, his strength. I couldn't get enough of him.

His hand clamped on my bottom, and he squeezed. Our kisses became deeper and wetter, and before I knew it, he'd rolled me under him, pressing his hard erection deep between my legs.

"You okay?" He slipped off one strap of my night-gown, exposing my décolletage.

I nodded. Better than okay. Best I'd ever felt in my entire life. Heat rose within me, and I experienced a raw pang in my core that I'd never felt before.

His lips made their way down my neck, delicately kissing my chest until he pushed down my slip. He grabbed my right breast, and I moaned as he sucked on it.

I threaded my fingers through his hair as his kisses turned more urgent— harder, rougher. His hand grasped my thigh, his finger tracing the hem of my panties, and I was afraid I was going to explode.

So, this was what I'd been missing all these years. Maybe he was right—sex *was* the most important part of a relationship.

I wanted more.

I wanted this; I wanted *him*.

But I couldn't possibly have sex with him. Not tonight. Not ever. It had been my choice to remain a virgin until my wedding night. I couldn't imagine sleeping with more than one man. Sexual freedom didn't extend to female members of the royal family. Honor was everything.

His mouth took my other nipple—and I went wild. My breathing quickened, and I writhed against him.

When his free hand slipped into my panties, I knew I had to stop him before I was unable to resist.

I forced myself to pull away from his lips, my body on fire from his touch. "I think that's enough kissing for tonight."

Tonight. There was only tonight.

Would I regret stopping this moment tomorrow? In a month? Forever?

His jaw clenched, and he finally exhaled. "Fine, Princess. Come here."

I could tell he was frustrated, but I appreciated that he didn't pressure me to go farther. He pulled me into his arms, and I rested my head on his chest. His fingers stroked my hair.

Would my fiancé ever kiss me the way Ryan had?

I didn't have to wonder, for my soul knew the answer.

No.

CHAPTER 7

RYAN

*T*HE NEXT MORNING, I WOKE WITH my arms wrapped around Giselle. My balls were in a world of hurt, but even so, spending the night with her had been worth it. Man, she was beautiful. Her long blonde hair fanned out over the pillow, making her look even more angelic.

I hopped out of bed and hit the head, hoping not to wake her. I resisted the urge to jump in the shower and jerk off. I'd never had a girlfriend and had rarely spent the night with a woman. I didn't even know what to do "the morning after" but bounce.

I wasn't willing to let her go today, despite telling her I would take her to her hotel. But it wasn't just because I wanted to fuck her. She intrigued me. When would I ever get another chance to escort a princess around France? What was the harm? It was only for a week, then she would run off and get married, and I would be nothing more than a distant memory of the time she went slumming with an American.

I emerged from the bathroom, and she was still asleep. I checked my email on my phone but found nothing important. I also scanned the news to make sure I wasn't a wanted man for kidnapping a princess, but luckily, I didn't find any articles about her, so I threw on my clothes and left the room.

The innkeeper waved at me, motioned me to wait, disappeared into the kitchen, and returned carrying a tray of food and coffee in a French press.

"Breakfast in bed for the newlyweds," she said with a wink.

I took the tray from her. "Thank you."

I went back to the room. Giselle had woken up and was standing at the window. I heard birds chirping outside and smelled flowers instead of my usual alarm of gunfire and smoke. I couldn't help but think how different this moment was from my day-to-day life. How nice it was. How normal.

She flashed a wide smile. "Good morning. How did you sleep?"

"Best sleep I've had in almost a year." I placed the tray on the bed, and she climbed back in with me. I pressed the coffee and poured her a cup, then served us both croissants. Mine tasted delicious, flaky and buttery. I ate a few berries, tried some yogurt, which tasted way better than the kinds I'd had back in the States, and finally dug into my cheese-filled ham omelet.

Giselle daintily nibbled on some berries. "So, what do you plan to do today?"

You.

"Hadn't thought about it. Just going to walk through town, check out the shops, maybe mingle with the locals."

"That sounds fun. Bayeux is a splendid town. It's less touristy here than in my country. I always imagined that it would be nice to have a summer cottage here."

Wow. It must be nice to just be able to buy property wherever you want. I considered a smart-ass, sarcastic response, but held back.

"Summer cottage? My goal is to afford one home

someday, not two, and on my salary, that will be a long shot, especially if I stay in San Diego. It's very expensive there."

A flush crept across her cheeks. "Oh, I'm so sorry. I hope you don't think I'm bragging. Forgive me. Do you like San Diego?"

"Love it. Miles of beaches, military city, laid-back vibe. I would never consider living anywhere else."

"It sounds lovely. I've always wanted to visit. I've been to New York but never made it out to the West Coast. Maybe you could show me around San Diego one day."

I glared at her. "With your new husband?"

She shook her head. "No. I will still travel alone on occasion."

Probably without security too. She just didn't get it. This—she and I—had a looming expiration date. I would never mess around with someone else's wife. Especially a royal. Best to just be straight with her.

"Well, based on what happened between us last night, I don't think that would be a good idea. You're like crack cocaine to me; I'll always want you. I'm in the military, honey. I don't want to be charged with adultery, especially with a princess. It would create an international incident. I can see the headlines now. 'The Princess and the SEAL: How a Summer Love Affair Turned into a Royal Scandal.' My CO would be on my ass, and it would ruin my career. *And* your reputation."

Her lower lip trembled. I decided to throw in a glimmer of hope.

"Of course, if you don't marry him, I'd love to show you a good time."

She answered weakly, "Oh, I'm getting married. Definitely. I'm so silly. Of course you wouldn't want to see me again. Sorry, I wasn't thinking. It just doesn't seem real to me yet. I'm sure I'll adapt."

The fact that she was describing getting married as "adapting" was heartbreaking. Well, it was her life. But she deserved more than a loveless marriage.

"I didn't say I wouldn't want to see you again. I said I *couldn't* see you again. There is a difference."

"Right. I get it. Well, instead, maybe I could show you around town today? And then I could check into my hotel later. There's really no rush. Once my father finds out what happened, I'm sure he'll make me return home."

Smart man. "Can't say that I blame him. I'd order you back home too. Hell, I'll go with you. Let me talk to him. I'll advise him on how to set up his own military."

"He'd probably love that. He really respects warriors. One of the reasons he wanted me to marry Miguel was to get some of the Quintana troops to create a base in Santa Cariña."

I laughed out loud. "That's ridiculous and absolutely not a reason to marry Miguel. Your father would be better off hiring a bunch of my retired SEAL buddies as contractors."

"That's an interesting idea. I'll suggest that to him. But I'm still marrying Miguel."

"Right, you keep saying that. Suit yourself, Princess." She was setting herself up for a life of misery. At least I was a straight shooter.

She looked out the window. "So, would you like to spend the day with me before I have to say goodbye?"

Goodbye? Fuck that, she wasn't going anywhere. But I wasn't going to tell her that yet.

"Yup. What do you want to do today?"

She blushed and crinkled her nose. "Me? I'm happy to do whatever you want."

I found her so incredibly adorable. She hadn't agreed to spend my entire vacation with me—yet. I wanted to make sure she had a good time with me, so that she would accept my offer later tonight.

I shook my head. "No, Princess. Tell me what *you* want to do with *me*. You seem to spend your life doing what people tell you to. I have the rest of my vacation to do whatever I want to do alone. You only have one day to spend with me. So how would you like to spend it?" I was using a trick I had learned in SEAL training, creating a sense of urgency to get better results.

"Are you sure? We could go to Omaha Beach."

"I'll do that later. Alone." Paying my respects to men who had died in battle was not my idea of a romantic day.

I wrapped my arms around her. I racked my brain trying to think of the perfect date. What did princesses like to do for fun? I honestly didn't know too much about her. Sure, I had studied her wiki. I knew about her charity work with children and her love for crocheting, but what really made her tick? "What's one thing you've always wanted to do that you've never done before?"

"I don't know. Let me think." Then she arched a brow. "Why are you trying to be so sweet to me, Ryan? You had this whole vacation planned, and I have already taken so much of your time. Why are you knocking yourself out to impress me?"

Good question. But I didn't have a good answer. "Stop asking so many questions, Princess. Your problem is that you think about everyone but yourself. You're constantly talking about your country, your father, your fiancé. I can guaran-fucking-tee that he isn't thinking about *you* while he's off sleeping with half of Europe."

Her bottom lip quivered again.

Fuck. I shouldn't have said that. I'd never had a filter. The truth hurt, and it was raw. I was sure she was surrounded by yes-people who told her what she wanted to hear.

But I came from a different world. A cold, dark reality where I took things as they came. Except in battle. When it came to war, I was always prepared and always one step ahead of the enemy to ensure my success and the success of my Team. But I doubted this strategic preparedness helped in areas of the heart.

"You're right. I know you are. It's just hard. I never really have free time. My calendar is always scheduled months in advance. I always go where I'm told, do what I'm supposed to do."

I may have been many things—insensitive, cocky, and pretty much an asshole—but indecisive was not one of them.

"Got it. Well then, I'm planning the day. Get dressed. I'll be right back."

She pursed her plump lips and nodded. "Okay. What should I wear? Are we going somewhere fancy? Or casual? Would shorts or a dress be more appropriate?"

Did she have someone lay out her clothes in the morning for her?

I would show restraint and not be a smart-ass. "Wear a sundress." I gave her a quick kiss and ran downstairs.

The innkeeper greeted me with a smile. "Monsieur Shelton. Did you like your breakfast?"

"Yes, we did. It was delicious. Thank you." I browsed some brochures near the front desk. Museums, history tours, train rides, the usual stuff. One caught my eye—skydiving. But I decided against it because I'd jumped off so many planes in my life, I didn't need the adrenaline rush right now, and I was sure Giselle would be terrified, which definitely wasn't my goal.

"Can I help you with anything?"

I never asked for help, but I didn't know the area, so what the hell.

"Actually, yes. I want to surprise my wife. We plan to do all the traditional tourist activities later in the week. Do you know of somewhere special to go to? Romantic? A hidden spot?"

She grinned at me and nodded. "Of course. I know just the place. There is a beautiful waterfall at the end of a short hike. I'll even pack you a picnic lunch."

Perfect. "Great. Thank you. Where is it? How do I get there?"

"It's about twenty minutes up north. Do you know how to ride a motorcycle?"

"Of course I do. I have a Harley back home."

"Well, then you can borrow my husband's. He would be thrilled to lend it to you newlyweds. He used to take me there when we were younger. May I ask how you met your beautiful wife? She looks very familiar to me."

That's because she's a princess.

I needed to figure out something after today. If she agreed to spend the next week with me, the paparazzi would definitely find us. The last thing I needed was my face plastered all over the international newswires so ISIS could put a bounty on my head.

"Classic damsel-in-distress story. She was being mugged, and I swept in and saved her. We fell in love. The rest is history."

She clasped her hand to her chest. "What a lovely story. Let me prepare your picnic basket. And I'll get the bike and helmets ready."

"Thank you. I appreciate it."

"Don't mention it. We are happy to help you celebrate your love."

I nodded. She was so nice. I wasn't used to such kindness. I wanted to take it at face value, but my past didn't allow me to do so. She was probably only being nice to me because I had booked this place.

I closed my eyes and shook off my anxiety.

No, Ryan. No.

Maybe she was just a wonderful woman who truly enjoyed making others happy. It was possible.

Man, I was fucked up. I hoped Giselle didn't know what a complete mess I was.

I raced back up to the room, opened the door—and my breath hitched at what I saw.

Fuck, she was fine.

Giselle was sitting there in a white sundress that ended right at her creamy thighs.

I wanted to climb on the bed, rip off her panties, and devour her pussy until she came all over my face.

My cock immediately stood at attention. How was I supposed to control myself around her?

Maybe I really *should* let her go after today.

I'd think about that later.

"So, where are we going? Is this dress okay?"

"It's perfection. *You're* perfection."

She giggled and pulled me onto the bed. I covered her luscious body with mine and pressed my cock between her thighs, with only the denim of my jeans and the soft lace fabric of her panties between us.

After a minute, I managed to push myself off of her and roll to my back. "Actually, you should change into some jeans if you have any."

"Really? Where are we going?"

"We're taking a motorcycle ride."

"I have never been on a motorcycle. Do you know how to ride one?"

I laughed. "Yes, babe. I own a Harley. You'll be fine. Just relax, and let's have fun today."

She climbed on top of me, and I grabbed her ass and kissed her like she was mine. Which she was. If only for today.

CHAPTER 8

GISELLE

A MOTORCYCLE RIDE? MY FIRST thought was to say no. He had told me to choose what to do, but I hadn't. This was all my fault. I was sure he would be okay with me picking another activity, but the main reason that I took this vacation was to be open to new experiences. So, I decided to force myself to go with the flow.

My hands shook as I followed him downstairs. Of course I'd never been on the back of a motorcycle. My father was way too cautious to allow me ever to endanger my life. He would absolutely flip out if he knew I was about to get on the back of a motorcycle with someone who was practically a stranger.

Giselle, stop! Your first thought is always what your father, your subjects, or your fiancé would think.

I closed my eyes; it was time to start living my life, doing what I wanted to do, and not stressing about what my father would say if he knew. After all, I was about to become a married woman. Surely I deserved some time to myself?

Ryan grabbed my hand, and we walked over to the innkeeper, who let out a dreamy sigh as we approached.

"Ah, the lovebirds. To be young and in love. Cherish this time."

Her words shook me. Would I have this much fun on my own honeymoon? What would I even do? I pictured awkward, painful, loveless sex, followed by me spending the day alone in the spa, sobbing while Miguel played poker in some casino.

What was I doing?

The innkeeper placed her hand on my shoulder, which brought me back to reality. And the truth was that today, I was still not married. And I was about to go somewhere with Ryan, my own personal bodyguard.

The lady handed me a picnic basket and beckoned us to follow her just outside the entrance. "I have prepared lunch and even added a bottle of wine for you lovers."

"*Merci beaucoup.*"

"*De rien.*"

She turned to Ryan and began giving him directions.

I shifted side to side on the gravel beneath my feet and pulled on my hair. Maybe this was a terrible idea. I really should just get to my own hotel. Going on this impromptu excursion was so reckless of me.

Ryan put his arm around me. "Let's go, babe."

Babe. No one except for Ryan had ever called me babe, not even my fiancé.

The innkeeper led us to the motorcycle. Ryan handed me my helmet and then strapped the picnic basket into the saddlebag.

Ryan adjusted my helmet for me and gave me a devilish grin. "Are you nervous?"

"Yes, actually, I am. I've never been on a motorcycle."

"You're going to love it—there's nothing like the

freedom of being out on the open road, the wind rushing through your hair, all your problems melting away."

That did sound lovely. I took a deep exhale and decided to give myself permission to take a risk. "I'll try to keep an open mind."

"That's my girl. Don't worry, babe. I got you. Just hold on tight."

Ryan put on his own helmet and effortlessly climbed on the bike.

Dear Lord, he looked so incredible in those jeans, which tightly hugged his sexy behind. I climbed on the back, wrapped my arms around his waist, and said a brief prayer as he revved the engine.

When he drove off, my heart raced. I'd never done anything like this in my entire life. I forced my nerves to calm down. As we took our first turn, the cracked pavement below us made the bike seem a bit unsteady. For the first few minutes, I closed my eyes and clung to Ryan for dear life. But as the road smoothed out, the rumbling in my heart gave way to pure bliss.

I was really doing it. I was living my life. Uninhibited. Wild.

I opened my eyes and took in the beauty of the moment. For the first time in my life, I was truly free. Free on the open road; free to enjoy my day how I pleased, and free to be me. I wasn't doing charity work or making a public appearance to promote tourism for my country. I was being selfish and indulgent.

And I had to admit, I loved it.

About twenty minutes later, we finally arrived at a meadow. Ryan helped me off the bike, and I removed my helmet.

"What did you think?"

"I loved it. I've never felt so free!"

His eyes twinkled. "Glad you liked it. I remember the first time I went on a motorcycle."

"Oh, really? When was that?" He sounded almost nostalgic. Maybe I could get him to open up a bit.

He looked away from me. "It was a long time ago, but I loved riding. I vowed to one day own my own bike. You should see mine back home—she's a beauty."

I pursed my lips. I had only known Ryan for less than twenty-four hours, but I was starting to notice a disturbing trend.

He hadn't told me anything noteworthy about himself.

Sure, he'd told me that he was a Navy SEAL, that he lived in San Diego, and that he never wanted to get married. But he had mentioned nothing about his family. I was dying to find out what his story was, but I had no right to ask. Especially since after today, we would never see each other again.

He leaned me against the motorcycle and kissed me, pressing his body into mine. This kiss differed from the previous ones we had shared. It was simple; it was sweet. It was the type of kiss I imagined a normal couple would share before going on a date. A couple who were dating because they both liked each other, not because they were being forced together.

"The innkeeper told me that there's a waterfall about a half mile from here. Are you game for some hiking?"

"Of course. A hike sounds fun. It's so beautiful out here." Fields of wildflowers surrounded us, and their bright pops of color plus the scent of the fresh air filled my heart with joy.

But after we began down the path, my jubilation was slowly replaced by concern. We were in the middle of nowhere. There was nobody else around for miles. No one knew where I was. I didn't even know where I was.

Yes, this was super romantic. A motorcycle ride out to a secluded location, complete with a picnic lunch and a waterfall. But I reminded myself again that I did not know Ryan, and he did not know me. For all I knew, he could be a psychopath. He could have lured me out here to rape me and leave me for dead.

Actually, the one thing I knew about him was that he had killed people. Nobody would ever know what had happened to me.

Oh my God! What was wrong with me? I was so paranoid—a complete mess. My chest heaved as my emotions and hormones took hold.

It was so difficult growing up the way I had. My entire life, I had been protected, sheltered, and controlled. Once my mom died, my father had become more protective than before. Now that I had this brief window with the freedom to do things on my own, I had zero confidence in my ability to take care of myself or to ascertain if people were telling me the truth.

My steps became slower, and I tried to focus on the beautiful deer grazing in the brush ahead . . . but anxiety took hold of me again, and I stopped dead in my tracks.

Ryan's head immediately snapped up, and he looked back at me. "What's wrong?"

"I'm just overwhelmed. That's all. Can we just take a minute?"

Ryan studied my face. I didn't want him to look at me to see what was inside, a weak mess.

He took my hand and motioned for me to sit down on a nearby fallen log, then sat beside me. "Babe, it's okay. I'm here. What's wrong? You can tell me."

I tried to gain control of my emotions, but I failed and began to cry.

Ryan just held me close to his chest as I sobbed. When I finally caught my breath, I looked up at him. He gently wiped away my tears.

What had I done to deserve this man? One of the few times I'd met Miguel, he was so annoyed by me when I'd been upset over how awkward we were toward each other. And Ryan, who owed me nothing, was just sitting here, being patient and kind to me for no reason at all.

"Sorry. It's just I never do things like this, ever. I'm never alone. I don't even know what it's like to be alone. My father or my chaperone is always around me. I just panicked because I don't even know you, and we are in the middle of nowhere. I shouldn't have come here; it was irresponsible. But I'm having a great time with you. Clearly, I can't even trust my judgment."

He rubbed my back. "I get it. You aren't being irrational, and I understand you're scared. I'm sorry I put you in this situation. We should've stayed in town around people, but I thought you'd like to do something different. I apologize. We can go back. I didn't mean to make you feel uncomfortable, Giselle."

Wow. He was so great. Still, a voice in my head whispered that he would drop me off at my hotel later today, and I would never see him again. Why would he want to hang out with me? I was a mess.

"Thanks for taking care of me. I feel so stupid. Everything you said about me yesterday was right. I can't believe I traveled here without protection. And please don't take any offense to this, but spending last night with you in a hotel was dumb as well. Coming here with you today to a secluded area where nobody knows where I am was also not the best idea. I don't even have any identification on me. I mean, you could literally be a serial killer, and I could die out here, and no one would ever find me."

Ryan put his arm around me, and I didn't push it away. "I'm sorry you feel that way, babe. I thought this would be fun. I guess I wasn't thinking about how you might get scared because I know that you're safer with me than you would be with anyone else. You're right. You shouldn't have come here alone with me when you had some doubts but you did, and I swear to you, I'm not going to hurt you. I don't expect you to believe me based solely on my word, though. If you want, we can get back on the motorcycle right now, and I'll take you wherever you want to go. Back to town and to your hotel, or anywhere else. Just name it."

I leaned into his chest as he stroked my hair. He was so kind and sweet, and everything he said reassured me that he was a good guy, but I wanted to find out more about him. Most men I'd met loved talking about themselves but Ryan didn't seem to share that trait.

"Can you tell me a little bit more about yourself?"

His shoulders tensed up. "What do you want to know?"

"Just more about you. About your family. Where are you from?"

He shook his head. "I don't know why it matters to you. You either trust me, or you don't. Me telling you about my fucked-up childhood doesn't change anything."

Yikes. Regret filled me. "You're right. I'm sorry I asked."

"It's okay. I just don't like to talk about it."

I nodded.

What had happened to him?

I wished he would open up to me, but our time together was coming to an end.

I appreciated that he didn't just lie to me and make up a story to answer my questions. Instead, Ryan had been careful about what he'd said.

I squeezed his hand. "Thanks for listening to me. I feel better. Let's go see that waterfall."

His hand cupped my face, and he kissed me. A sweet, gentle, soul-soothing kiss. The kind of kiss I had only dreamed about until now.

I still didn't know much about Ryan.

All I knew was that when I was around him, I felt safe and happy. And *seen*. Ryan looked at me the way no other man had ever looked at me. Somehow, I trusted that he saw the real me, the woman behind the princess.

CHAPTER 9

RYAN

$\mathcal{I}$ BEGAN TO QUESTION OUR PLAN as we hiked up to the waterfall. It hadn't even crossed my mind how taking this trip might possibly scare Giselle, probably because she had already spent the night with me. She didn't know a thing about me—and I wanted to keep it that way.

The view ahead was breathtaking: clear blue sky, endless lush green meadows, bright blooms, and wildlife frolicking in the distance. Sometimes when I was deployed to active combat zones, I forgot that places this spectacular existed. A peaceful area with no visual reminders of the hardships of war. I was so grateful to be here.

But the most beautiful view of all was her.

It sounded cliché, but it was true. Giselle was perfection. I hadn't lusted after a girl this much in years. Her sensual curves made my mouth water. I had to have her.

But honestly, what the fuck was wrong with me? Why was I delusional enough to think that a real-life princess would actually be interested in me? Of *course* she wouldn't be. She had even called me a vulgar SEAL, which was completely an accurate assessment. She was literally royalty. I was no prince—I was a jackass.

The only reason she'd spent the night with me was because she had nowhere else to go. Sure, she made out with me, but she was probably just looking for a little bit of fun before she committed herself to a loveless marriage.

Even so, I would stick around as long as she would have me.

Man, this full situation was so fucked up—just like the story of my life.

Her sweet voice jolted me out of my head. "I think this is it!"

She ran ahead to a clearing under a small waterfall.

The blue gush of water splashed into a small watering hole surrounded by rocks. This was no Yosemite, my personal favorite place for waterfalls, but it was pretty and peaceful. And the company couldn't be beaten.

Giselle skipped ahead. She was definitely the opposite of me. How her fiancé wasn't with her on this trip was beyond me—if she were mine, I would want to be with her all the time.

I placed a blanket down and opened the basket. The innkeeper had knocked herself out with the spread. There was an assortment of cheeses, bread, pâté, fruit, sandwiches, olives, and wine.

My thoughts turned to the innkeeper. What would it have been like to grow up with a woman like her as a mom? She probably packed lunches for her children. My mom had never done shit for me.

Giselle sat beside me. "Wow, this is so lovely! I feel like we are on a real honeymoon."

Ha. Except I still hadn't slept with the bride. I'd keep that comment to myself. "Well, I'd better enjoy it. This will be the closest thing I get to a real one."

Her beautiful smile faded. "Why do you say that? I know you say you don't want to get married now, but you're young. Many men marry later in life. Maybe you will change your mind when you meet the right woman. When you get out of the military."

"The only way I'm getting out of the military is in a body bag." I looked her in the eyes. "And maybe I've met the right girl, and she's engaged to another man."

Her bottom lip trembled. "Funny. You don't even know me. I'm sure you'd tire of me soon, anyway. Plus, we don't have much in common. Lust is not a good basis for a marriage."

"Ha. It's a better reason than giving your country a shitty military."

She grabbed a piece of bread and took a bite. "It's not just that. It's complicated. Our families go back for centuries."

"Got it, cupcake. So, it's about keeping your royal offspring pure and untainted with commoner blood."

She scowled at me. "Please do not put words in my mouth. It is not like that. Don't you get that I have nothing to do with this choice? Everything has been arranged. I don't get to say no."

"Then why do you say it's a choice? It's not a choice.

You're being forced to do this. You are a grown-ass woman—I don't care if you're a princess or not. You can call me an ignorant American if you want, but I would lay down my life for freedom—freedom of choice, of life, of religion, and yes, of whom to love. This isn't even about me; I'm not the marrying kind. Once we say goodbye, you'll never see me again. But you shouldn't ruin your life because you can't stand up for yourself. Mark my words, Princess, you will regret this 'choice' every day for the rest of your life."

Her jaw dropped open. Then she stood up and walked away from me, which was fine. I wasn't going to go after her, comfort her, and tell her everything was going to be all right because the truth was that it *wasn't*. I never sugarcoated shit.

I took a bite of my sandwich and chased it with a sip of wine. Guilt flooded me as I realized I had now ruined this perfect picnic.

Why had I even bothered?

Fuck. I shouldn't ever try to talk to anyone. This was why my way was the best. Love them and leave them. I was completely incapable of communicating with women. All I ever did was make them cry. I was such a bad boy that even my mom had left me. And none of my foster moms had wanted to adopt me, either.

A few more minutes passed, and I debated looking for her. This was definitely not how I had envisioned my vacation going. I should have already been balls deep in some chick, wasted on liquor, and having the time of my life. Instead, I'd somehow become entangled with a beautiful virgin princess, and now my cock was in a world of hurt.

Even worse, I couldn't stop thinking about her.

I took another swig of wine. Nope. I always saw a mission through. I would try to convince Giselle to spend more time with me.

Giselle finally returned. I expected her to chew me out but instead she looked apologetic.

"Look, I'm sorry I stormed off like a petulant child. Meeting you has rattled me. Before yesterday, I had accepted my destiny. I can't have you putting any doubts in my head. I think it's best if you just take me back to town, and we can say goodbye."

I laughed. *Not so fast, cupcake. I'm a SEAL—I never back down from a challenge.*

I pulled her down to the blanket and kissed her. Her greedy little mouth met mine kiss for kiss. She may be a virgin, but I knew there was a wildcat underneath her royal exterior. I couldn't wait to make her come, hear her scream my name, and beg me for more.

I wasn't going to let her go today. I ran *toward* conflicts, not away from them.

"Oh, forgot to tell you. Plans have changed. I've accepted your offer to be your personal bodyguard for the next week. I'm not letting you out of my sight until I leave this country."

CHAPTER 10

GISELLE

*W*HAT DID HE JUST SAY?

"No, that won't be necessary. I appreciate your offer, but I'm afraid I must decline."

"Too late. We're both looking for a good time, a care-free vacation. I don't speak any French, so you'll be an excellent travel companion. Do you really want to travel alone?"

No, I didn't. Initially, I'd thought it would be so free-ing, but I had to admit that being mugged had flus-tered me. "No. But I don't want to ruin your trip. I'm sure you want to hook up with some gorgeous woman."

"I plan to. You. So what do you say?"

I stared at this handsome man next to me. What was I doing? I couldn't possibly travel with him. What if someone took a picture and leaked it to the tabloids? What if my father found out? Or my fiancé?

Or, even worse, what if I fell madly in love with this man?

One week of passion followed by a lifetime of regret. A fun fling would be one thing, but I was already developing feelings for him. There was no way I could risk that.

"No. I'm sorry. I can't. I don't want to create a scandal. And aren't you SEALs supposed to remain hidden? If we're discovered together, your name will be reported in the press."

"If I can evade terrorists, I can evade photographers. No one needs to know my name. Worst-case scenario, if a picture gets out, you can tell people I'm your bodyguard."

He kissed me again, his rough stubble scraping my chin. My mind flashed back to last night when he had kissed me everywhere. I was dying to make out with him some more. But I didn't know if I would have the strength again to tell him to stop.

And despite waking up in a SEAL's bed, I had no walk of shame to take. I was so turned on last night when we were kissing that I had seriously considered losing my virginity to him. He seemed to really like me—did he? Or was I just a challenge?

More importantly, did I fancy him?

The answer to the latter was yes, yes, and oh, yes, but it didn't matter. I had to be calm and rational. Detached.

Royal.

"For a whole week? Where will we go?"

"We can stay here for a few days, visiting the war sites. And I loved this ride so much that I was thinking I could rent a motorcycle, and we could ride through the countryside and find some small towns to explore."

Motorcycle? Today was one thing, but traveling all around France on a motorcycle? My father would murder me. What if I got injured?

I refused to tell Ryan my first thought was of my father because it would feed into his perception that I was incredibly sheltered and overly concerned with what everyone else thought of me.

A perception that was completely accurate.

"And then what? After what happened last night, I'm sure we will become more intimate. I mean, what I'm saying is, last night was wonderful. You want to take me on a romantic escapade around this country and then never see me again?"

"Well, I don't have a choice in the matter, do I? You're getting married next month, and I'll be deployed again somewhere in the Middle East. In a way, the lack of any possibility of having a future together makes this easier on both of us, don't you think?"

"I guess." But I knew he was right. We had no hope of a future together.

I was promised to another man. He was promised to another country.

But we could always have France.

The gravity of this decision weighed heavily on me. On the one hand, I believed this was the wrong thing to do. Foolish, actually. I barely knew this man.

On the other hand, if I said no to this romantic rendezvous, I would likely regret this decision for the rest of my life. I would always wonder what kind of love affair I could have had with this American hero.

"So, what do you say?"

He kissed me again and pushed me back to lie under him on the blanket. I could feel his hard erection pressing against my thigh. He interlaced his hands with mine as his lips ravished my body.

I writhed under him, waves of pleasure pulsing through me. Ryan was electric. I couldn't believe how ridiculously sexy this man was. Prior to meeting him, I had found my own fiancé mildly attractive, but now, after being kissed by this masculine man, I didn't think I could ever be satisfied by Miguel.

I came up for breath. My heart fluttered, and my fingers tingled. "Yes. I'd love that."

"You won't be sorry, Princess. You're looking for adventure, and I'm the right man for the job."

CHAPTER 11

GISELLE

ANTICIPATION MIXED WITH ANXIETY inside of me. I was going on a wild adventure with this sexy man. I couldn't wait to get started—but first, I had to call my father.

He most certainly would be panicking after not being able to reach me on my cell or at the hotel, even though I had emailed him and told him not to worry.

I turned to Ryan. "We should get back. I need to contact my father."

He smirked. "What are you going to tell him?"

"Just the truth."

"And what's that?"

"That I lost my phone and purse. But that I've decided to continue the trip."

"Lost?"

I rolled my eyes. "Yes, lost. He doesn't need the morbid details of my mugging."

Ryan shook his head. "Lying won't help anything."

I didn't need a lecture from him. "It's fine."

He nodded. "So, no mention of me, huh?"

I exhaled. I didn't want to hurt his feelings, but he could never, ever understand the pressures of my life.

Then again, I could never understand the stress of his. Out at war. Being shot at. Killing people.

I shuddered.

"No. It would be best if I didn't mention you. It would be a thing. I hope you understand." I closed my mouth. I wasn't going to tell him that I had snuck downstairs last night while he was in the shower and emailed my father. Even worse, I had already lied to my father by saying that I had run into an old female friend and had merely lost my phone. Ugh, I was the worst. Already lying to cover my tracks. I felt like a naughty teenager.

I wasn't a teenager, though. I was an adult woman. And I had made a choice to travel with Ryan.

I just wished I didn't have to tell my father.

"Yup. Let's get going."

We quickly packed up the picnic. I looked longingly at the waterfall; so peaceful, so serene. I yearned to come back here again and enjoy the beauty in its simplicity. That was what I craved—living in the moment and finding pure happiness, not constantly worrying about the future.

Sadly, that type of life would never be my reality.

Ryan secured our picnic items in the saddlebag on the motorcycle and climbed on the bike. I straddled the seat behind him and wrapped my arms around his waist. I breathed him in as if he were a drug. My ultimate high.

The engine roared to life, but unlike our trip here, this time I felt calmer. I was certain about what I was going to do: enjoy the remainder of my vacation with this beautiful stranger and then, when it was time to say goodbye, walk away with no regrets.

We finally arrived back at the bed-and-breakfast. Ryan and I thanked the innkeeper for letting us borrow the motorcycle and for packing us the most delectable picnic.

Ryan brushed a lock of hair off my face. "Do you want to use my phone to call your dad?"

I shook my head. "No. Let's go to my hotel. Not to check in, but to call him from there. Then we can return here to stay."

He frowned slightly but said nothing, and I was grateful that he didn't argue with me. I wanted no more tension on this trip. Just happiness. Just peace. Just romance.

We walked through town, and Ryan held my hand. His firm grip guided my steps on the cobblestone streets. I leaned closer to him, inhaling his scent. We hadn't even known each other for more than a day, and I was already getting used to being with him.

Before I knew it, we arrived at the hotel. Ryan opened the door for me—and I gasped.

My father was standing there, pacing around the lobby.

Oh no.

I turned to Ryan. "That's my—"

"Father, I know."

My face scrunched up. "How do you know?"

"Because I memorized everything I could about your country last night. Regular intel for planning a mission."

Right. I was a job to Ryan. A challenge. Sure, he was attracted to me, but he seemed to have some misguided sense of duty to protect me. But Ryan's mission plans were the least of my worries—I had to focus on my father.

The king.

My father's eyes immediately met mine. He motioned for me to come toward him.

Uh-oh. I could already tell I'd royally pissed him off.

I squeezed Ryan's hand. "Let me handle this."

"I'm going with you."

My heart softened toward Ryan. Most men I'd met would run away from any conflict, yet he was offering to stay by my side.

"No. That won't be necessary. Why don't you stop at a café for some coffee? I'll meet you back at the bed-and-breakfast."

Ryan shook his head. "No. I'll wait for you. I'll just sit here."

He grabbed a newspaper and sat on a sofa in the lobby. I was impressed that he hadn't bolted the first chance he had.

I walked toward my father. The second he glared at me, guilt covered me like a blanket. The deep lines around his eyes seemed even more prominent as he scowled.

But I knew that he wasn't going to yell at me in public. We were royals, after all.

He pointed toward an office. Great, he must have already secured a room so he could scold me in private.

Head held high, I greeted him with a curtsy and a kiss on his cheek.

"Giselle! Where have you been? No one has been able to get in touch with you. We contacted all of your friends from university and no one had seen you."

Shame consumed me. This was entirely my fault. I knew that my father would worry. I had placed myself in this situation. I needed to take full responsibility for my foolish actions.

"I'm fine, Papa. I'm so sorry for causing you to worry. That was never my intent." I needed to come clean now. "I'm sorry I lied to you in my email. I didn't merely lose my phone; I was mugged in the town square yesterday. Luckily, I met a gentleman who went after the criminal and retrieved my luggage."

My father's jaw dropped. "A gentleman? Where is this gentleman?"

"He's in the lobby."

"You said you stayed with a friend. A female friend. That was a lie? Please tell me you didn't spend the night with some man you met on the street."

Well, when you put it that way, it really does sound awful.

My cheeks burned from embarrassment. "I did, in fact.

I had no money or identification, and I didn't want to alarm you. Nothing happened between us at all. He's a Navy SEAL, an American. And quite a gentleman."

The second those words left my lips, I knew that I'd just walked into a ring of fire. I had admitted that I'd spent the night with Ryan.

My father's hands shook. "Giselle, you stayed with an American assassin? What were you thinking? You are engaged to be married! Young lady, how foolish could you be?"

Normally, I would just allow my father to have the final word.

But not today.

"I was thinking, Papa, that I had just been mugged, and I was terrified. This man, whom you just called an American killer, was actually the only person in this entire town to ask if I was okay. He ran after my mugger and attempted to get my items back." I paused —about to lie. "Absolutely nothing inappropriate happened between us. I'm completely lucky that I met him. You should be *thanking* him."

My father glowered at me, and I met his gaze right back. I was not going to back down.

"Why didn't you just walk to the nearest hotel and have them call me? I would have wired you money immediately."

Good question. I didn't want to tell him the truth. Which was that I'd seen the past twenty-four hours as a brilliant opportunity for a once-in-a-lifetime adventure with a handsome stud. One that I would never regret.

"Well, honestly, Papa, it was late, and I was scared. I was pretty shaken up after I had been mugged. And I really didn't want to bother you or have you worry. I took this trip to become independent and enjoy my last days as a single woman. The last thing I wanted to do was run to my father and ask for help."

My father exhaled. "I understand, Giselle. I just wish you had been honest with me. So, what are your plans now?"

Breathe, Giselle, breathe. "I plan to continue my vacation."

"Very well. But I must insist on providing you security. Pierre and Henri traveled with me. Henri can stay behind with you."

I didn't want to travel with Henri—I wanted to travel with Ryan.

"I appreciate that offer, Papa, but I have to do this on my own."

My father shook his head. "No, Giselle. I insist. See what happened when you traveled without protection?"

I nodded. "Yes, I do. And that was wrong of me. But I want to be alone, away from the palace and everything that goes along with it. Just for a little while." I paused and closed my eyes. "I've hired the Navy SEAL as my own personal bodyguard for the rest of the trip."

His eyes bulged. "An American? No. Our security detail is fine."

I silently doubted Henri or Pierre would've handled the mugger the way Ryan had. "Well, it's not up to you, Papa. This is the last time I can be on my own before my wedding. I'm continuing my trip with Ryan."

"That's completely out of the question. In case you have forgotten, young lady, you are engaged to Miguel. It's inappropriate for you to be traipsing across the country with an American man."

Heat stirred inside me, and years of anger and resentment pulsed through my words. "And what, pray tell, is Miguel doing at this exact moment? Last time I checked the tabloids, he was on a yacht in Ibiza with a bunch of models. I'm not married yet and so I will do what I want, when I want. I'm sorry I worried you, but I assure you that I am fine, and my virtue is intact. You will see me back at the palace in a week, but until then, I'm going to continue my trip with Ryan as my bodyguard. That's final." A wave of relief rolled off me as I said those words.

Wow. I couldn't believe I actually stood up to him. I had always been the dutiful daughter and proper princess. What had possessed me to stand up for myself?

One word.

Ryan.

I had only known him for a day, and I was already asserting myself.

My father locked his eyes on mine. I had his stubborn streak; he knew that all too well. I would not back down.

"I must meet this young man."

Right. Ugh. Meeting the parents was a bit too soon but Ryan wasn't my boyfriend, he was my bodyguard. Although Ryan had already offered to talk to my father, so I was sure it would be fine.

"Of course. He's in the lobby. I'll go get him."

I walked out to Ryan, who was staring at his phone. His eyes lit up when he saw me, and warmth flooded my body.

"How'd it go? Do I need to kidnap you from your castle in the middle of the night?"

I rolled my eyes. He was always such a smart-ass. "My father wants to meet you."

"Cool, I'm always down to meet a king. Let's go."

Ryan's self-confidence amazed me. Most men were nervous to talk to my father.

Ryan stood up, and I couldn't help but sigh. He was so handsome and rugged. And completely not my type. But at least he did look like a bodyguard. I hoped this would work.

We walked into the room, and my father gave Ryan the once-over.

Ryan bowed when he saw my father. "Honored to meet you, Your Majesty."

I melted, pleasantly surprised Ryan had shown my father respect.

My father's stern look widened into a smile; he always responded well to deference. Then he extended his hand out to Ryan. "Thank you for watching out for my Giselle. I appreciate your help, but we are no longer in need of your services as we have our own security. Please let me know what I owe you."

Oh no.

Ryan's jaw clenched.

I put my hand on his as if to urge him not to speak, but I was too late.

"May I ask where your security detail is?"

My father frowned. "No, you may not. Young man, my safety, and the safety and well-being of my daughter is none of your concern."

Ryan let out a laugh, and I cringed as he pointed to Pierre, my father's personal bodyguard, who was lounging on a chair. Henri was busy chatting up a maid in the corner. Ryan eyed him as well. "Those guys?"

My father nodded. "Yes, actually. They are the best in my country."

"The best? I walked into this room with you, the *king*. He didn't even frisk me. I could be armed . . . but I don't need to be. I'm a Navy SEAL—I've killed men with my bare hands. Some bodyguards they are. If I were your bodyguard, I wouldn't allow anyone to get near you without being properly vetted."

"Well, fortunately for me, you are not my bodyguard. A brash, impulsive American cowboy such as yourself would most certainly cause an international incident."

My eyes watered. I couldn't even watch this train wreck. I grabbed Ryan's hand, but he kept on talking.

"I completely disagree that you're no longer in need of my services. Your daughter, the crown princess, was traveling alone in a foreign country where she was mugged by two assailants. And I saved her. She has informed me that she would like to continue the excursion she had planned and offered me a job as her security guard. An offer which I accepted, despite being on my own vacation."

My father narrowed his gaze at Ryan. "That is absolutely out of the question." He glanced at me. "Young lady, you can continue your trip with Henri, or you will return to the palace at once. It is your choice."

Ryan opened his mouth. "Doesn't sound like much of a choice to me. Sounds like an ultimatum. Like the rest of her life 'choices.'"

No one ever stood up to my father.

And now Ryan had.

My turn again.

"No, Papa. I will be continuing this trip with Ryan as my personal bodyguard."

A slight grin graced Ryan's face. "Please don't worry about your daughter. I promise she'll be well taken care of, and I will not harm her or disrespect her or your country in any way. You have my word. I can leave you my information as well as the contact numbers for my military command. I can authorize them to send you my qualifications and the details on my numerous combat medals."

Now was my chance. "Bye, Papa. Please leave the copies of my identification, my credit cards, and my passport with the concierge." I gave him a kiss on the cheek. His fists clenched, and confusion and rage swirled on his face.

I turned and walked right back out of the hotel with Ryan trailing behind me.

CHAPTER 12

RYAN

I GRABBED GISELLE'S HAND ONCE we were outside of the hotel. "Are you okay?"

She leaned into my chest, and I embraced her. "No, of course I'm not. Thank you for backing me up though, it means a lot to me. No one has ever defended me to my father like that."

That's because you've never dated a real man. "No need to thank me, babe. I was so proud of you and the way you stood up to your father."

And I was, but I knew that it was a onetime thing for to stand up to her father about a quick vacation before she was married. She would never stand up to him in the long term. No matter what happened between us in the next week, she would definitely go through with her marriage next month.

Not that it mattered to me. I'd known her for only a day. Why should I care who she married? One thing was for certain—she would never marry an American like me.

"Yeah, I did. I think I really made him upset. But he had no right to come after me and demand I return home. I just knew he would do this; I knew that he wouldn't trust me to be on my own."

I smirked. I didn't want to agree with her father and upset Giselle, but even so, I felt the need to be honest with her. I could tell that like most privileged girls I'd met, Giselle spent her life surrounded by yes-people who would never call her out on her shit.

I would always tell her the truth, no matter what it cost me.

"I mean, I can't say that I blame him. I would've come after you too."

She gritted her teeth and pulled away from me. "I'm an adult. Why does everyone treat me like I'm a child?

My father, Miguel, and now you? I can handle myself."

I exhaled. That did not come off the way I'd intended.

"I understand, babe. I'm not saying that at all. I know you can handle yourself, but like I've been saying, you're royalty. He was obviously worried, and rightly so." I needed to change the mood. I put my thumb under her chin and forced her to look at me. Her mascara was smudged under her eyes, but I still thought she was the most beautiful woman I'd ever seen. "So, what do you want to do now? Go out to dinner?"

She shook her head. "Actually, no. I'd like to just rest and order room service."

I paused. We were staying at a small bed-and-breakfast. I didn't think they *had* room service, but I could ask.

"Sure, whatever. I'll ask the innkeeper if she can make us dinner, and we can eat in our room." Her face contorted. What was on her mind? "What? What are you thinking about?"

"Nothing."

"No, it's not nothing. What are you thinking?"

She dropped her shoulders. "Seeing my dad rattled me. And I told him you were my bodyguard. Now that he knows about you, I don't think we should lie."

"I'm not following you, babe."

"Is there any way we can stay at my hotel? I have a suite with two separate bedrooms."

"My place is fine."

"But it's really not, Ryan. If word gets out that we are sharing a small room, it could be really damaging to my image."

I exhaled. I knew this was coming. Now that her father knew that I would be traveling with her, I would have to guard not only her but also her reputation.

I had given my word to her father, so I might as well man up.

"Fine. Let's go check out."

She placed her hand on my arm. "Thank you. I really appreciate it."

"Don't mention it."

We walked down the street in silence. I was careful to keep my distance from her while I scanned the area for any suspicious people. Once we arrived at the bed-and-breakfast, I had the awkward talk with the innkeeper. She had been so kind to us that I didn't want her to think we hadn't enjoyed her place. I paid her in full for my week and explained that Giselle wanted to be in the center of town.

As I carried our luggage back to the château, I began to have doubts about what I had agreed to. What on earth was I doing playing bodyguard to some pampered virgin princess? I wasn't even going to get laid on this trip, and now I was working during the vacation I'd dreamed about for the past seven months.

I quickly squashed my desire to ditch her. I had agreed to this, and I always finished what I started.

We checked into the château, and Giselle was pleased to know her father had done as she'd asked and left everything she'd requested with the concierge.

The bellman led us to the suite. I entered and took in its opulence. It was nothing like my cozy room back at the bed-and-breakfast. There were crystal chandeliers, velvet curtains, sculptures, and artwork. There was even a grand piano in the middle of the room. Too bad I couldn't play.

It was still cool as hell—I could get used to this.

The bellman tapped me on the shoulder.

"Pardon, *monsieur*. Your room is across the hall."

Oh, hell no. "I'll be staying with Princess Giselle; I'm her bodyguard. There are two separate rooms in this suite."

"Her room has secure locks and an alarm. I was given strict instructions by her father, King Rémy, that you are to stay in the room across the hall." He handed me my key.

Giselle turned to me, a look of distress plain on her face. "I had no idea. I—"

I put up my hand to stop her from completing the sentence. I'd expected this. "It's fine. I'll sleep there. Good night, Princess. Enjoy your room service."

And with that, I went into my room. Alone. Just how I liked it.

Well, usually.

CHAPTER 13

GISELLE

THE NEXT MORNING I WOKE refreshed and ready to face the day.

I felt awful that the bellman had asked Ryan to stay in a separate room, but it had given me the space I'd needed to think. After taking some time alone, I was surer than ever that traveling with Ryan was the best decision I had made recently. I needed this excursion. And for now, I needed him.

I just hoped Ryan wasn't having second thoughts about traveling with me. I wouldn't blame him if he was. I couldn't help but feel like I was ruining his vacation.

But today, I would make it up to him. I had the whole

day planned. We were going to see the Normandy beaches. I had already arranged for a tour guide and limousine to take us.

I ordered a full breakfast to the room and got ready. I picked the prettiest sundress I had packed, curled my hair, and put on my makeup. I was full of joy for no reason at all; all I knew was that I wanted to look good for Ryan.

I was about to leave the room and knock on his door when I heard a rap on my own. It was probably room service.

I pulled open the door—but it wasn't room service. It was Ryan, who looked as handsome as ever.

Except for that scowl on his handsome face.

"Good morning. Why are you so sour?"

"Why did you open the door? You didn't even ask who it was. I could've been some stalker."

Ah, Ryan. "You are so paranoid. We are in an exclusive hotel, and no one knows I'm staying here besides you and my father and the staff. Anyway, I thought it was room service; I ordered breakfast. Come inside."

"Are you sure? Your father won't be too mad if I'm

alone with you, will he? I can wait in my room. Or even in the lobby, if you'd prefer."

His condescending tone didn't go unnoticed by me. "Stop, Ryan. I'm sorry about that. But I do think it's for the better. We really shouldn't be spending the night together. It is inappropriate."

Ryan smirked and then pulled me into his arms. "So that's it, huh? I'm just your bodyguard now?"

My heart beat strongly. I should say yes, that was all he was. That was the honorable thing to do.

But I didn't want to be honorable; I wanted to be bad. "No, Ryan, that's not it." I tilted my head, offering myself to him, and he didn't hesitate to kiss me.

He slammed the door shut and pressed my back against the wall, kissing me like he had been dreaming of kissing me all night.

Had he?

He hiked up my dress, and his hand gripped my thigh. "I missed you."

"I missed you too."

This passion and heat were unreal. I had always believed this kind of chemistry only existed in movies.

I was glad I was wrong.

Ryan's hands were sliding under my dress and up my legs when there was another knock at the door.

"Room service."

Ryan grunted and then released me. I straightened out my clothes and peered in the mirror—my lipstick had smeared—the truth about my bodyguard was written all over my face. How embarrassing.

Ryan opened the door, grabbed the trays from the guy, and placed everything at the table.

His eyes widened when he saw the food. I had ordered almost everything on the menu because I wasn't sure what Ryan liked. I hoped he didn't think I was showing off—I didn't know how else to repay his kindness.

Ryan shoveled some eggs on his plate and doused them with hot sauce while I poured him coffee.

After a few bites of food, he seemed to relax. He winked at me. "So what do you want to do today, babe?"

"Oh, I booked us a tour of the Normandy beaches. We have a chauffeured limousine and a private guide. It will be great."

Ryan raised his eyebrow. "A limousine? A private guide? No thanks. I'd prefer to just go low key."

My chest constricted. Had I made a mistake? I was just trying to do something nice for Ryan, and it had backfired on me. "Oh, I'm sorry. I just thought it would be nice to go with an expert."

"It's really not my style, but thanks. I appreciate the thought."

I knew I shouldn't push, but I couldn't help myself. Ryan was so stubborn and prideful. Why was it so difficult for him to accept kind gestures from anyone? It probably had a lot to do with his childhood. I needed to stop prying into his past. "Are you sure, Ryan? The guide is a war historian. Very knowledgeable. Could you at least try for me since I already paid? I promise you will have a great time. But if not, I understand."

Ryan's eyes met mine. Maybe he wasn't used to people doing sweet things for him, but I wanted him to know he could trust me. "Hmm. Well, in that case, let's just take the tour. Since you already booked it."

Gotcha. "Yes, it would be easiest." I beamed and he grinned at me in return.

We finished our meal and then headed downstairs to meet the limo. Ryan checked the limousine driver's identification and made sure it matched the itinerary. Wow. It must be exhausting to be that thorough and paranoid.

I climbed into the back of the limo first, then Ryan raised the divider and put his arm around me. I nestled against his chest. It was nice. Very romantic but very chaste. I had spent my life traveling around the world, but usually only accompanied by my chaperone or my father. I enjoyed having someone by my side with whom I could share new experiences.

The drive was breathtaking, and the beauty of the French coastline mesmerized me. I imagined honey-mooning here, with a view of the ocean.

But when I closed my eyes, I pictured Ryan by my side, not Miguel.

I was clearly irrational. Ryan would most definitely not be going on my honeymoon.

I looked over at Ryan, who didn't seem to be having the same reaction to the view that I was. His eyes were red and watery.

I placed my hand on his thigh. "What's wrong?"

"I just imagine all those young men seeing this coast as they rushed off the boats, knowing they were going to die."

My chest constricted. I had always considered myself so cosmopolitan, but Ryan saw the world through a completely different lens, one I could never understand.

How could I lead my own country if I didn't understand the hardships of the world?

I kissed him on the cheek. "You are amazing, do you know that? I'm so glad I met you."

He cupped my face and kissed me back. "I'm glad I met you too. And I need to thank you. I have never in my life traveled like this—the château, the limousine, the private tour. It's really nice to have someone to experience this country with."

And with that, we melted into each other and made out like we were teenagers.

CHAPTER 14

RYAN

Y EYES BEGAN TO TEAR WHEN I stared at the ten thousand perfectly aligned crosses. They were placed in formation, like little soldiers, on a cliff overlooking Omaha Beach.

The crosses were pointed toward America.

I choked up. Though I had read many books about the war, being in the cemetery rattled me. I knew that I risked my life every day as a SEAL and that I, too, could end up sacrificing my life for the freedoms of my country.

Just like Giselle was sacrificing her happiness for the sake of her own country. The irony about what we had in common was not lost on me. I loved my country; she loved hers. And this love would ultimately keep us apart.

The escort was chock-full of information. Some of it I'd picked up over the years from various books and documentaries, but a good amount was still new to me. Despite my initial reluctance to take a guided tour, I was grateful that Giselle had hired him.

As Giselle and I walked hand in hand through the memorial, I saw an old man wearing a cap that had *D-Day Survivor* stitched on it.

I extended my hand to him. "Sir, I'm so honored to meet you. I'm a Navy SEAL, and I'm completely in awe of how brave you were here. Thank you for your service."

He smiled and shook my hand. "Thank you, young man. I appreciate your kind words, but it still feels strange to be thanked for the worst day of my life."

His reaction caused me to pause. I saw him as a hero, and even though he was revisiting his past, the pain of his memories was evident in his sad eyes. How many friends had he lost here that day? What had he seen?

"I understand, sir."

He glanced at Giselle. "Is this beautiful lady your wife?"

I winced. He must've seen her ring. "No, sir. Unfortunately, she is not."

He placed his hand on my back. "Son, I fell in love with a girl once. She was beautiful. A nurse. Hair the color of sunshine and eyes the shade of rain. But I didn't want to get married while I was in the army. When I returned, she had eloped with someone else. I never forgave myself for letting her go." He looked again at Giselle then gave me a knowing look.

I nodded. "Thank you, sir. It was nice to meet you."

His words seared me deeply. Would I regret letting Giselle go? But unlike this man, I didn't have a choice in the matter. Giselle was engaged to another man. Someone of royal birth, while I was just a literal bastard.

But even in the few days since I had met her, I realized that I wanted more out of life.

Maybe I would like to have a girlfriend.

Too bad it would never be Giselle.

Giselle placed her hand on my chest. "I'm sorry about

that. I should take off this ring, but I keep it on in case I get photographed. I hope you understand."

Right. Those pictures could be explained away. After all, I was just the help, her bodyguard. "I get it."

My heart was overwhelmed with death and sadness. We finally left the memorial and headed back to the hotel after an exhausting day. I felt satisfied that I had paid my respects to the men who had sacrificed their lives for freedom. The greatest generation.

By the time we got back to the château, we were both wiped out after our long trip. Giselle had even fallen asleep on me for part of the ride home.

She stood in front of the door to her room. "Would you like to come in? We can order dinner and watch a movie."

I exhaled. Normally, of course I would. But I wasn't in the right mindset after what we had seen today.

"I'd love to, Princess, but I'm going to call it a night. Today was rough for me. I just need to be alone."

She looked down at her feet. "I understand."

I lifted her chin and kissed her. "Good night, Giselle."

"Good night."

I surprised myself by telling her no, but I wanted to think about the day we had just spent together. I went to my room and ordered room service and liquor. The more I drank, the more I started to relive my darkest memories. I could feel my foster dad's hand around my throat, smell his tobacco-laced breath, hear my foster sister's cries for help. The cocktail of alcohol and death consumed me until I passed out.

The next morning, I woke with a wicked hangover. Despite that, I felt a little better and brighter. I grabbed a quick shower and pulled myself together.

I really regretted not sleeping in Giselle's room last night. We only had a few more days together. What had I been thinking?

Now that I had achieved my goal of seeing Normandy, I wanted to have some fun with Giselle. This was my vacation. So far, she had been mugged, we went on an emotional picnic, she received a lecture from her daddy, and yesterday we took a trip to a cemetery. Man, I really knew how to show a girl a good time.

I knocked on her door, and she opened it.

She smiled when she saw me. No one ever smiled when they saw me. "Did you sleep well?"

"No. But I feel better. What did you want to do today?"

"I was thinking we could walk around town and see the Bayeux tapestry."

I loved that she was finally making plans and not just going along with what I wanted to do. "Let's go."

I was eager to explore Bayeux, especially with Giselle as my company. We stopped for breakfast at a local café. Giselle ordered for us in perfect French. A few people seemed to stare at us, and I wondered if they recognized her, but no one said anything to her. Plus I hadn't seen any more paparazzi.

After a delicious breakfast, we walked to the museum.

Giselle took my hand. "The Bayeux Tapestry shows the events up until the Norman conquest of England. It's simply gorgeous."

I was in awe of the vast cloth which depicted epic battles. Swords, shields, and soldiers stitched in remembrance. To think this was the way these warriors' lives were immortalized warmed my soul. It was truly a stunning piece of art.

And I was grateful to see it with Giselle.

We strolled through some more exhibits with Giselle narrating as we went.

"How do you know so much about art?"

"Oh. I studied it at college."

"Right. You went to the Sorbonne?"

"Yes. It was glorious. *J'adore Paris*," she said, sounding wistful.

"I've never been."

Her eyes lit up. "Oh, we must go. The nightlife, the food, the museums; it's my favorite city in the whole world." She bit her lower lip once she realized what she'd said. "I mean, you must go. Someday."

Her words weighed on her. I wanted to go to Paris. When I'd originally planned this vacation, I figured I'd try to swing a quick stop after seeing Normandy. Now I wanted to go with her. But our time was running out.

After our day date, Giselle went back to her room to freshen up. I ordered a bottle of champagne, flowers, some strawberries and chocolates, and a cheese tray and knocked on her door.

She greeted me wearing a sexy dress.

I was obsessed with her body. This was the longest I had ever been around a woman romantically and not slept with her.

I was starting to see the problem with my past. I had always assumed that I was just a player. Keeping people away from me ensured that I didn't get hurt.

But, and I hated to admit it to myself, I actually enjoyed being around Giselle. I liked the way she asked how I was feeling. She had tried to do something nice for me with the tour, and I had a great time at the museum today.

This was her last vacation before her marriage—I needed to do something great for her as well.

She beamed. "Hey, handsome. You brought me flowers?"

"Yeah. I wanted to thank you for today and yesterday. It was really nice of you to arrange the trip for me."

"Don't mention it. It was nice of you to offer to be my bodyguard and not ditch me after you met my father."

"Well, it wasn't completely altruistic."

She smirked. "Oh, really? Why is that?"

"Because I'm crazy about you."

I put down everything I was carrying and pushed her against the wall. She didn't resist and met me kiss for kiss, stroke for stroke. I felt the outline of her panties through her dress, and I was dying to rip them off and taste her pussy, but I held myself back.

Why was I so drunk on her? Why this girl? Why now?

Fuck. I pulled myself off her. "Sorry. I can't resist you."

"Don't apologize. I love kissing you."

But I wanted more.

I brushed her hair out of her face. "Hey, why did you say we should go to Paris?"

She shook her head. "Forget it. It was a slipup."

"Wait, now you don't want to go with me?"

"No, I do. It would still be fun. But . . ."

I took her hand and gazed into her eyes. "But what? Tell me."

"This may seem silly, but I have always wanted to go to Paris with a boyfriend. I've never had a boyfriend and I know I'm engaged, and it's weird and all, but I'd love to go to Paris with you. We could stroll along the Seine, dine at a romantic bistro, visit the Louvre, kiss at the top of the Eiffel Tower. Well, maybe not that since a ton of paparazzi are certain to be there. Still, I think we could have fun." She looked at me shyly.

Paris is for lovers.

I didn't even know where I'd heard that phrase, but it rang in my head.

And maybe, if I took her to Paris, we would become lovers.

At first, taking her virginity seemed like a sleazy goal, even to me. But now, there was more to it. I liked her . . . I cared about her.

I wanted to know what it would be like to sleep with someone I had feelings for. Until this trip, I hadn't even known that I was capable of *having* feelings for a woman; back in San Diego, I was deployed continuously. Even if I wanted to start a relationship with a girl, I never had the time.

Well, I still didn't have the time. We had less than a week together. I had to shoot my shot or I'd regret it.

I grabbed her hand and pulled her closer. "Let's go."

She bit her lip. "To Paris? Now?"

I leaned in and kissed her again. This time more intimately, slower, lovingly. My cock was so hard it was painful. I needed her.

"Tomorrow morning. With me. Let's go fall in love."

CHAPTER 15

GISELLE

*P*ARIS! I COULDN'T BELIEVE RYAN was taking me to Paris. This was my dream come true. How did I get so lucky?

Getting mugged was a blessing, not a curse.

I booked a romantic hotel in the heart of Paris. Ryan had wanted to find a bed-and-breakfast, but he quickly relented when I emphasized the need for extra security in Paris. I found his Achilles' heel quite useful.

Next was to call my father and inform him I would be heading to Paris. He seemed slightly annoyed but didn't say anything else. I assured him that Ryan was behaving like a perfect gentleman, and we would be getting two rooms, all of which was true.

The next morning, Ryan insisted on renting a car and driving to Paris. I would've preferred to take a limo, but I wasn't going to argue.

After a quick stop for lunch, we finally arrived in Paris and checked in.

"So, where do you want to go first?" I'd been here plenty of times before, so I wanted Ryan to take the lead. This was his vacation, after all.

"I've made a reservation at a restaurant with Eiffel Tower views. I hope it's up to your standards."

Ah, he was so adorable. "You don't have to impress me, Ryan. I'm just happy that I'm here with you." He smiled and leaned close for a kiss. It was just starting to get good when he pulled away.

"Babe, I need to run an errand. I'll be right back. Don't leave this room or open the door under any circumstances."

Again with the paranoia. "I'm fine. Why are you so convinced I'm in danger? No one knows I'm here."

"Don't start with me. Kim Kardashian was robbed in Paris, and she's just a reality TV star. You're a princess. And you were mugged. Just listen to me. Please. I'll just be downstairs."

"Fine. I will stay put." I had to trust he had a good reason for all of this. He kissed me again. "Lock the door behind me."

"Yes, bodyguard."

And now I was alone. Time to get ready for my date.

I spent some time picking out an outfit—a sexy dress and high heels. I laid it out on the bed and decided to bathe.

I drew myself a bath and added some bubbles. Before I stepped into the hot water, I looked at my naked body in the mirror. My entire life, I had been self-conscious; my thighs were too big, my tummy wasn't flat. But for the first time, I felt not just beautiful but sexy. Ryan couldn't keep his hands off of me, and he was gorgeous. It didn't seem to be an act, either. He truly wanted me.

Maybe I *should* lose my virginity to him.

I slipped into the bubbles and allowed my mind to roam. Ryan's words rang in my head. Why did Miguel get to have all the fun? Why couldn't I enjoy and explore my sexuality?

I soaped myself up and pictured Ryan. A raw pang filled my belly. I wanted him. He wanted me. Why didn't I go for it? No regrets. Just enjoy myself for the little time we had left together.

I rubbed my nipples and began to feel a throbbing between my legs.

Then I heard a knock on the door.

"Babe, open up."

I knew what I should do: hop out of the tub, dry myself off quickly, throw on some clothes, and answer the door.

But I didn't want to.

I climbed out of the bath and raced to the door, *naked*. I peeked through the peephole to make sure it was Ryan.

It was.

"Babe, are you there?"

You can do this, Giselle. There is nothing wrong with wanting him. Miguel doesn't deserve your virginity.

I took a deep breath—and opened the door.

Ryan's jaw dropped, and his eyes bulged as he took in my naked body.

Ryan stunned me as well.

He was wearing a designer suit and carrying red roses.

One look at me and he dropped the roses, slammed the door shut, and carried me to the bedroom. "Are you playing with me, Princess?"

I shook my head. "No, I'm not. I want you."

And I meant it.

He pushed the clothes I had laid out earlier off the bed and quickly undressed but left on his boxer briefs.

"You looked so sexy in the suit," I said and pouted.

"Fuck the suit," he said in a low growl.

"Don't we have dinner reservations?"

"We can be late. I'll eat *you* instead."

Ryan's lips touched mine, and I sucked in a breath. He bit my bottom lip. This one kiss could last me a lifetime of loneliness. It was the type of kiss that writers in this very city wrote novels about. But this kiss wasn't fictional; Ryan was here. And he was mine. For now.

His hand moved to cup my breast. My naked skin tingled with pleasure. How could someone from the other side of the world know how to make my body feel so good?

I gasped as he rubbed his thumb over my nipple. My body was on fire, and the throbbing between my legs grew deeper. I was desperate to feel him inside of me.

His tongue quickly replaced his thumb. I moaned as he kissed and sucked on my tits.

"Oh, Ryan!"

His hand slipped down between my legs, softly caressing me. No one had ever touched me there, and the strength of his hand sent shivers through me.

His eyes met mine with a devilish grin as he kissed his way down my body.

Nerves rattled inside me. I tried to pull his head up. "Ryan, I've never done that."

"I know. It's okay. Do you want me to stop?"

"No, I'm just nervous. I may not like it."

He laughed. "Oh, you'll like it, baby." He spread my legs wide. "You have the most beautiful pussy."

Hearing his words made me feel so dirty, but in a good way.

I shouldn't be doing this. I should stop.

He licked me slowly down my center, and the foreign sensation drove me wild. He made small strokes with his tongue as he settled between my thighs, and I arched my back in ecstasy. I stared at him pleasuring me, and the sight sent me to heaven. I closed my eyes and gave myself over to the moment. This was nothing like I thought it would be. I feared I would hate it, or it would be awkward, but it was nothing like that. In a word, it was absolute bliss.

His tongue felt incredible. Pleasure built inside me. I felt like my legs would give out.

"Do you like it, Princess? Do you like it when I lick your pussy?"

I nodded.

"Say it, Princess. Or I'll stop. Tell me what you like."

"Don't stop! I love it."

His mouth covered me, and he licked and sucked some more. I couldn't possibly have ever imagined anything feeling as good as Ryan's mouth felt on me. My breath quickened, and I felt like I was going to explode.

I looked down, and Ryan was lapping me up. Just seeing this gorgeous man pleasing me sent me over the edge.

"Oh my God, Ryan. Yes!"

A rush of euphoria covered me as I came, pure joy filling my body.

Ryan pulled himself up to kiss me on the forehead. "How do you feel?"

"Incredible." I paused and stared at his hard erection through his boxer briefs. I still hadn't seen him naked. "Can I do something to make you feel good?"

He shook his head. "I feel great."

I looked at him, perplexed. "I can try to suck on you. I'm sure I'll be bad."

"That's not even possible, babe. I'd love to, but not tonight."

Hmm. "Okay." I climbed on his lap, rubbing myself on him. "Make love to me."

He exhaled. "I don't think that's a good idea."

His rejection stung. "Wait, you don't want to have sex with me?"

He stroked my hair. "I do, babe. More than anything. But I don't think we should."

I frowned. "Why? What we just did was pretty intimate."

"Save something for your husband. Once you sleep with me, you'll never want another guy. I don't want to ruin you." He grinned.

I hit him with a pillow. "You're impossible. Let's just have sex!"

"No."

What? "Why? I thought you wanted me."

"I do. I just . . . I just think it's a bad idea."

I couldn't let this go. "Why? You clearly have had sex with many women. Why won't you sleep with me?"

He looked at me, a sad expression on his face.

"Because I actually like you. And I think you'll regret it. I admit, I initially wanted to seduce you and bounce, but I'm trying to do the right thing here."

I didn't even know how to respond to that. But my heart broke.

What was I doing with this wounded man? He seemed so strong and tough on the outside, but inside, he was sad and alone. He was developing feelings for me, and I was just using him for some prewedding fling.

I was just the worst person.

"Are you sure? I want to, Ryan."

"Yeah, I'm sure. Let's get ready for dinner."

He grabbed his clothes and walked into the bathroom.

A wave of guilt washed over me, not just for getting intimate with Ryan, but for playing with his emotions.

I ached for him. I wanted him to feel as good as he'd just made me feel.

And I knew that no matter what, I would miss him when he was gone.

CHAPTER 16

RYAN

*W*E HAD A ROMANTIC DINNER, but my mind was elsewhere. What was wrong with me? Giselle asked me to blow me, hell, to take her virginity—and I had turned her down.

Why? I loved sex; it was my favorite vice. I'd always been down to sleep with women without a second thought. *Wham, bam, thank you, ma'am.* Why was I stressing about this one chick?

Why had I said no? I was losing my game.

But I *did* know. I'd even told her. Feelings. I was having feelings for her. I never had feelings; I had closed that part of my heart off years ago.

Ever since my mom OD'd, I'd been hesitant to trust

people. The few times I briefly let anyone in other than my Teammates, I'd been destroyed. Never again.

The next day we woke early and had a long day of sightseeing. Giselle covered her hair with a scarf to avoid being recognized. She took me to the Louvre, where we saw the *Mona Lisa*. My mind was utterly blown that I was actually going to museums in Paris with a princess. I would've never in my wildest imagination thought that this would be my life right now.

After another intimate dinner where we dined on coq au vin and sipped a magnificent merlot, Giselle and I strolled along the Seine River.

The view of the Eiffel Tower after sunset was spectacular.

I cupped her face and kissed her under the moonlight. "I'm crazy about you."

I was truly happy for once in my life. Even if we only had one night left together.

Was this what my buddies talked about when they wouldn't shut up about their wives? And if I was really falling for her, why did she have to be taken?

I held her hand as we walked down the gaslight-illuminated street. We approached a corner, and Giselle stopped cold.

I looked up and saw a dimly lit man with his arms around two women wearing tight dresses and fuck-me heels. Giselle looked like she was about to cry.

"What's wrong, babe?"

"That's . . . that's Miguel."

Oh, *hell* no.

Miguel noticed us looking at him and whispered something to the women. They nodded in unison and moved away from him.

Giselle stepped forward and shed my arm.

Got it. I was the help.

"Giselle, darling." He walked over to her and kissed her on the cheek.

Rage seethed inside of me. His designer purple suit and shiny black shoes clung to his scrawny body. I wanted to throw him into the river.

"Ladies, this is my fiancée, Princess Giselle. Giselle, these are my 'friends.'"

The brunette bounced over to Giselle. "Oh, hi! We've heard so much about you. I love Santa Cariña. Miguel said he'll be running the casinos. I can't wait to come visit. I've never been friends with a princess before."

What a mindfuck. What planet did these people live on? I felt like I was on some fucked-up version of the *Royal Bachelor*. I'd rather be fighting ISIS.

"Hello, Miguel. This is Ryan. He's my . . . bodyguard."

Knife. Heart.

But that's all I was. Her hired hand. I knew my role: be her bodyguard, protect her, take her to dinner, make her come.

Then walk away.

Maybe it was the red wine, or maybe it was just because I was a hellion and looking for a fight, but I couldn't hold my tongue.

"Well, since you two lovebirds are engaged and all, we should just leave you alone to celebrate your engagement. I can call your 'friends' a cab. Hey, Princess, maybe you and your fiancé can spend the night together in your suite."

Giselle placed her hand on my chest, her eyes

pleading with me. "Ryan, stop. You knew I was engaged. Please don't make a scene."

I turned to her, blood pounding in my ears, my mind slamming shut all the doors to my heart. "Yeah, I knew. But I didn't think I'd meet him."

Miguel laughed, then whispered something else to one of the girls. She giggled.

He touched Giselle's arm. "Is there a problem, Giselle? You seem to be quite cozy with your bodyguard."

I pointed in his face. "Watch it, buddy. I'm warning you. You don't know who you are talking to."

But that motherfucker didn't back down. "Dude, it's okay. Not sure if Giselle told you, but we aren't together romantically. It's an arrangement. Maybe you can teach her some tricks. Just break her in for me, would you? I'll thank you later."

That was it. Fuck this dude.

I clenched my hand into a fist and clocked him in the jaw.

"Ryan!" Giselle jerked away from me to rush to Miguel's side.

Fuck that. Fuck her. Fuck my promise to her father. If she wanted to waste her life with some scumbag like Miguel, I should just let her.

I stormed down the street, not knowing where I was heading. I just wanted to get out of Paris, out of France, back to the USA.

And forget I ever met this princess.

CHAPTER 17

GISELLE

"*R*YAN! WAIT!" I SCREAMED AS I raced after him. I kicked off my heels and tried to catch up, but he was almost half a street ahead. Wow, he ran fast.

I kept sprinting and finally got closer to him. "Please, Ryan, let's talk."

He finally turned to me, his face flushed, his eyes wide. "Why? What do you want to talk about? How you're about to marry a guy who doesn't even respect you? Wants me to 'break you in.' What kind of man says that? What a worthless piece of shit."

I glowered at him in the moonlight. "You're one to

talk. You said you've been with hundreds of women. You are no better than he is."

"Fuck you, Giselle. How dare you say that? Yes, I am better than him. My previous women wanted nothing more than I did. They were hookups, one-night stands. They meant nothing to me, and I meant nothing to them. I've never had a girlfriend—I've spent more time with *you* than I have with any other girl."

"More time? Less than a week?"

"Yes, smart-ass, less than a week. And I would never, *ever* want to share you. Just the thought of that sleazy motherfucker touching you makes me want to kill him." His lip trembled, and I could see his breath in the air.

"You care that much about me?"

He looked at his shoes. "Yeah. I guess I do."

"I do too."

"It doesn't matter anyway. I'm leaving tomorrow."

There was an awkward pause. Then a crazy idea hit me.

"Well, maybe I could go with you."

His eyes met mine. "With me? To San Diego?"

"Yes. Why not? I have another week of vacation. I've always wanted to visit the West Coast."

He gritted his teeth. "What's the point, Giselle? We should end it here. Now. I'll just call your dad and get Henri to watch you. Nothing good can come of this affair. Let's just call a spade a spade and go our own ways."

I touched his face, trying to bring him back to me. "But I don't want to. I like you."

He stared at me, and I felt him coming back to me. "I like you too. But we have nothing in common, and you're about to marry that douche canoe back there. I'm out."

He turned and continued down the street, but I ran after him again.

I grabbed his shoulder. "No, listen. It will be fun. Why can't we just enjoy the little time we have together?"

"Do you always get your way? Never mind. Don't answer that."

I pouted. I knew I was spoiled, but I wanted Ryan. "Fine, Ryan. I can call my father myself. But first look me in the eyes, and tell me you never want to see me again. This is your last chance because I will be married next month. To Miguel. Say goodbye if you want, but leave me with no regrets."

His eyes met mine.

Checkmate. Ryan wasn't one to back down from a challenge.

"Fine. You win. Come back to San Diego with me. I'll show you a good time." He pulled me to him and held me close. "But I'm warning you, Princess—one more week with me, and you will never want to leave."

CHAPTER 18

RYAN

*H*OW DID THIS GET SO INTENSE, so fast? I had *always* lived my life with no regrets. And I did have another week of leave back in San Diego. I could show off my princess to my friends.

And then she would leave me forever.

But I wasn't going to focus on that now.

Giselle booked a ticket back with me and, of course, upgraded us to first class. I was starting to get used to her fancy lifestyle. She would probably refuse to stay at my small apartment. Maybe I should book her a suite at the Del. Royalty always stayed there, and it was right next to the base.

Our flight was long, but at least we got to sleep on the plane. Our seats even reclined flat, and the food was surprisingly good. I never thought I'd ever have a decent meal on an airplane. Most of the time I'd spent in planes was with a parachute strapped to my back, and a gun slung across my chest.

I was still livid about Miguel. And Giselle wouldn't even talk about it with me anymore. She kept telling me that their marriage was set in stone. And since I didn't want a relationship with her, it didn't matter.

But was that true? Was I certain I didn't want to be with Giselle? She was on my mind twenty-four hours a day. Would I ever get over her? Or would I be dreaming about her for the rest of my life while I was stuck in some fighting hole overseas?

Probably the latter. Fuck. But what was I going to do about it? What *could* I do about it? Not only was she engaged but also, she was a princess. She could never be satisfied with me or my life.

So I would spend this week with her, and then we would say our goodbyes. Forever.

I woke before our plane landed in San Diego, and she

was nestled under my arm, sleeping contently. She looked like an angel.

Fuck, I was whipped.

I roused her from her sleep. "Babe, we're almost here."

She rubbed the sleep out of her eyes and sprang up. She gazed out the window toward the sunset. "Oh, it's gorgeous! Reminds me of Santa Cariña. Maybe you—"

She didn't complete her sentence. We both knew what she was going to suggest. We also both knew that it would never happen.

The plane touched down, and we disembarked. I gathered our luggage and stepped away to call my good friend Erik, who was waiting in the cell phone lot to give me a ride home.

He picked up on the first ring. "Welcome back, buddy. How was it?"

"Crazy. Hey, you alone?"

"No, Dax is with me."

Dax, the rock star turned SEAL. That dude was even more of a womanizer than I was. I didn't want him anywhere near Giselle. At least Erik was a solid guy and married; his wife was an Olympic gold medalist and the first female Navy SEAL. She was a complete badass.

"Well, heads up, I'm not alone."

"What? You brought some chick home from Europe?"

"Yeah, actually. And she's not just a chick. She's a princess."

He laughed. "Aren't they all?"

"No, seriously, dude. She's a real-life princess. Princess Giselle of Santa Cariña."

"How the fuck did you meet a princess?"

"She was getting mugged, and I saved her. She's also engaged. It's complicated."

He laughed again. "Damn, man. I knew you shouldn't have gone alone. Hell, even Dax could've kept you out of trouble."

Now it was my turn to laugh. Dax got more pussy than the tiger exhibit at the Wild Animal Park here in San Diego.

"Just be cool. And tell Dax to behave. We'll be outside in a few minutes."

"Gotcha."

I headed back over to Giselle, who looked effortlessly beautiful. I took our bags, and we went outside.

A few minutes later, Erik pulled up in his huge truck. He and Dax hopped out, hugged me, and threw our luggage into the bed.

Dax walked over to Giselle and knelt before her, his hand across his chest. "At your service, Your Royal Highness. Would you knight me?"

Giselle smiled at me. "Your friends are charming."

I shook my head. "No, they're not; they're jackasses."

I opened the front passenger seat for Giselle and climbed in the back seat with Dax.

"So, a real-life princess. I've actually been to Santa Cariña, it's a beautiful country."

Of course he had. I wanted to roll my eyes. Dax had been everywhere.

She turned her head to look back at us. "Really, when?"

"Ten years ago. When I was on tour."

"Tour? A military tour?"

He shook his head. "No. I was in a band. I doubt you ever heard of us."

And that would be all he would say. Dax never told *anyone* that he wasn't just in any band. He was the former lead guitarist of Gold Whiskey, one of the biggest bands of the millennium.

But that was his secret to tell, not mine.

"Do you want to come over to our house for dinner? Aria cooked up a feast."

I didn't want to tell Erik no, that I wanted to keep Giselle to myself a bit longer. With all of Aria's endorsements, they purchased a beautiful home in Coronado right next door to Dax's mansion, which he bought with his rock star money. I didn't want Giselle to see their places before she saw my tiny digs.

"We're a bit jet lagged. Maybe in a few days."

"Sounds good."

Erik soon pulled up outside of my apartment. It was

small but homey. Unlike Giselle and these guys, I didn't have any money. I came from nothing. Anxiety consumed me.

It didn't matter how hard I was falling for Giselle; she was way out of my league.

CHAPTER 19

GISELLE

*T*HE NEXT MORNING, I WOKE UP exceptionally early due to the time change. I snuck out of bed before Ryan was awake. I wanted to make him breakfast, but his refrigerator was bare. Maybe later on we could go grocery shopping together. Instead, I brewed some coffee and snooped around his place.

He had a few pictures displayed, one of him at his Navy SEAL graduation, and another with his friends.

But he had no pictures at all of his family.

Nor had he ever talked about them.

Why was he so secretive? I had no idea who this man I was spending so much time with was. Nothing about his parents, or if he had any siblings. What was his story?

A few minutes later, Ryan emerged from the bedroom wearing nothing but pajama bottoms.

My eyes bugged. He was so gorgeous; I couldn't handle it. He could be a movie star.

"Morning, babe. Sorry that I don't have any food here. I always clean out my fridge before I deploy or go on long trips. Let me take you to breakfast. Did you decide what you wanted to do today?"

You. But that wasn't in the cards for me. Ryan had made it very clear that he didn't want to have sex with me. Well, he did, but he wouldn't. He was still pissed off about Miguel's "break her in" comment. So was I.

Did I have to sleep with Miguel? Maybe we could just agree to a sexless marriage. When we needed to have children, we could use artificial insemination.

Just considering those awful thoughts made me nauseated. How could I go through with this? How could I never see Ryan again?

I shook the thoughts of Miguel out of my head. "I wish

to go to the zoo. It's supposed to be one of the best in the world."

"It is. Although, I've never been."

"Really? How is that possible? You live here."

He shrugged. "I never had anyone to take. And I don't have much free time. I'm always training or deployed."

Right. Ryan was a workaholic. Then again, so was I. I was always going to a charity event, a state affair, or a fundraiser. It was rewarding work, but sometimes I craved a simpler life.

Every year, when I went to our summer cottage, I had the most splendid time. I spent my days tending to the vegetable garden and my nights reading books by the hearth. I learned to cook many dishes from various cuisines. Nowhere to go, no one to see. Just peace and happiness.

I wished I could take Ryan there.

"Well, I can't wait to explore the zoo with you."

"Zoo it is. I'm going to hop in the shower."

He didn't ask me to join him. I wanted to but didn't.

When Ryan was done, I took my own shower and then got dressed.

We had a quick breakfast at a local café and headed off to the zoo.

When Ryan handed me a map of the zoo before we started, I knew I had underestimated my shoe choice. There was no way we'd get through the whole thing in one day. I had never seen anything like this. The animals were kept in huge enclosures with ample land to roam. Koalas were my favorite animal, so we started there.

The koalas clung to their trees, eating their eucalyptus leaves.

I clasped my hands to my chest. "Aren't they adorable? I love them. Australia is lovely."

"Really? I've always wanted to go."

I resisted the urge to again suggest we could go somewhere together. Instead, he kissed me right in front of the koalas.

Click.

My head jerked back. Some lady was taking a picture of us with her phone. Had she recognized me?

"Sorry to startle you! You both just looked so happy, so I thought I'd take a picture. Here, I can airdrop it to you."

Ryan smiled. "Sure. Thanks."

Ryan held his phone up to hers and magically, the picture appeared.

I stared at the photo, and something struck me.

I had never seen myself look so happy before in my life.

Ugh. Would I ever be this happy again?

We strolled through the rest of the zoo. The hippos and the gorillas were other favorites of mine so we went to see them next.

After a long walk, we finally stopped at the food court to get a snack.

In front of me, a young couple gave their toddler daughter an ice cream cone. The father looked so caring . . . just like Ryan.

My heart ached. I felt like I was facing an oncoming train and was powerless to stop it.

"What's wrong, Princess?"

"It's just . . . I want that." I pointed to the couple.

"An ice cream cone? Chocolate or vanilla?"

Ryan could definitely be clueless sometimes. But it was adorable.

"No, silly. *That*. A family."

Ryan scowled. "Well, I'm sure you and Miguel will have beautiful children."

"Stop, Ryan. I know. You've already told me over and over what an idiot I am. My marriage will be loveless. Miguel is a jerk. I'll regret it. Don't marry him. *Stop*. I'm not going to change my mind."

"You're right. I won't waste my breath. Nothing I say changes anything. You're going to do what you're going to do, no matter what I say." He stared at the family and then turned his head. "I'm ready to bounce."

"Okay."

We left the zoo behind, and along with it, my dreams of a happy little family.

CHAPTER 20

RYAN

*T*HE NEXT DAY, I TOOK GISELLE FOR a tour of the base. I was so proud to show her off but embarrassed that she wasn't mine.

She was engaged to another man.

But Giselle was charming as always, and the fact that she was a real-life princess fascinated all the SEALs.

We had brunch at the Del, and then she shopped at a few boutiques. I dutifully carried her bags. Man, who was I?

We finally left and went back to my place. The second we were inside, Giselle wrapped her arms around my neck and kissed me. I ripped off her dress, and she stood in front of me wearing nothing but a lace bra and matching panties.

God, I wanted to fuck her. And she kept asking me to. Why was I still holding back?

I was about to pick her up and carry her to the bedroom when she flipped the script.

She knelt in front of me, tugging on my belt buckle.

"Babe, you don't have to."

She nodded. "I know, Ryan. I want to. I want to please you. Please, let me."

This woman, this princess, was begging to suck my cock. Even a saint couldn't keep holding out like this.

Time to give in to my desires.

"Only if you ask me."

She bit her lip. She was definitely not used to dirty talk.

"I just did."

"Tell me what you want to do. I want to hear you say it."

She exhaled, her voice low and sweet as she said, "I want to suck your cock."

Ah. Hearing this good girl, this virgin princess, say "cock" alone was almost enough to send me over the edge.

She undid my belt, my shorts fell to the ground, and she pulled down my underwear.

Her beautiful blue eyes looked up at me.

"Ryan, you are huge."

God, I loved this girl. "Say that again."

"No, seriously. What should I do? Sorry, I'm super sheltered."

"Don't apologize. I love that you've never done this before."

"Really?"

"Yes, really. Grab me, baby. Rub your hands up and down over it."

She obediently did as I asked. Her delicate hand felt so soft against my cock.

"Like this?"

"Just like that, baby. Now, put me in your mouth."

Her eyes widened, and those beautiful lips of hers parted. The anticipation was killing me. Ever since I met her, I'd been so sexually frustrated, but I'd put my desires aside. I never wanted to pressure her at all.

She planted a kiss on my tip as my cock grew harder in her hands.

"Don't be shy. Suck it, Princess."

She didn't hesitate and took me completely in her mouth.

Her warm tongue felt heavenly. As her head bobbed up and down on my cock, I gave myself over to pure bliss.

"That's it, baby. Don't stop."

My breathing became labored. I ran my fingers through her hair, guiding her rhythm. One more look down at this beautiful woman pleasing me threatened to send me over the edge.

I pulled her off of me. "I'm going to come."

She immediately took me back in her mouth. Hell, I warned her.

She sucked me tightly, and pleasure ripped through me. I exploded in her mouth. I was certain she was going to run to the bathroom and spit, but instead she swallowed.

Damn.

I put on my underwear and then sat beside her, stroking her hair.

"I hope that was okay. I didn't really know what I was doing."

Her innocence broke me. "It was perfect. Giselle, you are perfect."

CHAPTER 21

GISELLE

*T*TOOK ANOTHER GLANCE IN THE mirror. I was so nervous about going to Erik's house. I had already met him, and he seemed lovely, but I was eager to meet his wife, Aria. I had read everything about her online. She was an Olympic gold medalist in synchronized swimming, one of my favorite sports, and she was the first female Navy SEAL. I was so impressed by her.

We pulled up to a glorious mansion on Ocean Avenue. I couldn't help but notice that there was a For Sale sign on a property a few houses down. I didn't dare inquire about the price because I didn't want Ryan to feel uncomfortable with my wealth. Besides, what was I going to do with a home in Coronado? Stare out the window at Ryan running past me on the beach while I wept?

Aria opened the door and immediately embraced me. "Princess Giselle, it's so lovely to meet you."

I presented her with a bouquet of flowers. "Likewise, Aria. And please, call me Giselle. Thank you for having us."

Erik handed Ryan a beer.

Ryan touched my arm. "Babe, I'm going to go help Erik barbecue. You good?"

"Yup. I'm great."

He kissed me on the cheek before heading for the grill.

Aria's dog sniffed my toes.

"Flounder! Stop. I apologize for him. He's a beagle, which is pretty much a nose with a dog attached."

"Oh, no worries at all. I love dogs. I have a Cavalier King Charles Spaniel myself."

She smiled. "Can I offer you a drink? Wine? Lemonade?"

"I'll have the lemonade. Thank you."

She led me into the gorgeous kitchen. It was so light and bright. Miguel had said he wanted to live in the palace after we got married, but I would prefer something simpler. Not that Miguel cared about my preferences.

Aria motioned for me to have a seat at the island. "So, is this your first time in San Diego?"

"Yes. I love it here."

"Yeah, you can't beat Coronado. Though I hear you have fabulous beaches in your country."

"We do." I paused. She had obviously researched Santa Cariña. She had to know about my engagement. I took a deep breath and said, "You must think I'm so awful, coming here with Ryan. I'm sure you know that I'm engaged."

She poured me a glass of lemonade, added a sprig of lavender, and then stirred it before handing it to me.

She sat down beside me. "I don't think you're awful at all. I can't even imagine what it's like to be a royal. I'm sure you have responsibilities and commitments that I can't even begin to understand."

"I do. Don't get me wrong. I love my life. But my duty

comes first. This is the first time I have traveled alone. Ever."

She nodded. "I don't want to make you feel bad, but Erik has mentioned to me that he has never seen Ryan like this. He's crazy about you. He never dates. Like, ever."

Guilt ate me up inside. "I know. He's told me. I'm crazy about him too. I wish I were free to love him, but I'm not."

I gazed out at the ocean. I wanted so badly to break away, be free, live my life by my rules, but I just couldn't. The invites were sent, the wedding was planned. How could I bring such shame to my country?

Aria placed her hand on mine and offered me a sympathetic smile.

"I get it, I do. But secrets will eat you up. And you deserve to be happy. I really hope everything works out for you."

"I appreciate that."

Erik called us for dinner. We dined in the backyard. Two couples just talking about life and sharing laughter without a care in the world. I had nothing like this back home. My cousin was great, but she was more of a party girl. My friends from university were busy with their own lives. I craved to be part of a real group of tight-knit friends.

But genuine friendship and true love were two luxuries I couldn't afford.

CHAPTER 22

RYAN

GISELLE INSISTED ON COOKING dinner. We went to a local fish market, and she picked out all the ingredients, making an incredible salmon dish with asparagus and potatoes. I was impressed that she could cook, but Giselle was full of surprises.

After dinner, we relaxed and had a glass of wine. It felt good to be alone with her in my place. Like we were a normal couple, even though we were anything but.

If I was being honest with myself, I was getting used to having her around.

She placed her hand on my thigh. "Can I ask you a question?"

"Shoot."

"Tell me about your family."

Anything but that.

"Why?"

"Because I'm curious."

"But why does it matter?"

"Because this is what people do, Ryan. Talk. Express themselves. It's not healthy to keep your life bottled up inside."

My internal shield popped up as if I was going to war. I inhaled and exhaled slowly, allowing my SEAL training to take over and counteract the heat in my chest. "Why? You aren't my girlfriend. You won't be with me at the dock when I deploy or greeting me when I return. Why should I tell you anything?"

She bit her lower lip. "Because I care. I'm sorry my life is the way it is. But I still care about you. I will always care about you. Let me in."

Fuck. What did I have to lose?

Oh yeah, my heart.

Maybe it would help me to share. I had never told a soul about my past. Not even my Teammates.

I took a deep breath, willing my hands not to shake.

"Fine, Giselle. My mom was a crack addict. Fucked so many men that I don't even know who my father is, because she sure as hell never knew. I'm a fucking bastard. She overdosed, and then CPS took me in. I was in the system my entire life. No one wants to adopt a little boy who's a troublemaker. So, I got passed around to foster home after foster home. And I was abused. Daily. I watched my foster sister get raped. I tried to save her, but my foster dad beat the shit out of me."

The second the words left my mouth, I instantly regretted them.

Giselle clasped her hands over her heart and looked at me with a combination of pity and horror. She would never see me the same way again. As her hero. I was beneath her. Definitely not suitable to date royalty.

She reached out to me, but I pulled away. "Ryan, I'm so sorry. I shouldn't have asked."

"Yeah, you shouldn't have. Look, I'm going to call it a night." I went to my room and closed the door. Fuck. I was being a jerk. She was just trying to get close to me, but I couldn't help myself.

Why had I let her in?

After my foster dad burned his cigarette into my neck, I vowed to be the biggest, baddest motherfucker in the world so no one would hurt me again.

But I hadn't succeeded. Because someone was about to hurt me.

And that person wasn't a motherfucker the size of a pickup truck.

That person was a beautiful princess.

CHAPTER 23

GISELLE

I CLIMBED INTO RYAN'S BED LATER that night after giving him some time alone to cool off, but he was passed out. I tossed and turned beside him until I fell into a fitful sleep. The next morning, we didn't talk about his past. It was so horrifying; I didn't want to pry further. I regretted asking him to open up, especially because he was right. No matter what, I was going to leave.

We spent the day lounging on the beach, and the sun and saltwater seemed to help lift our spirits. Ryan even taught me how to surf. I'd always been so scared to learn, but with Ryan by my side, nothing seemed impossible.

Back at his place, I relaxed on Ryan's sofa. He turned on Netflix, grabbed a beer for himself, poured me a glass of chardonnay, and put his arm around me.

I glanced around his small apartment. The coffee table was spotless, and he even had some cozy throws draped on the back of the couch. I closed my eyes— what it would be like to live with him? Could I get used to the simple life that I'd always proclaimed to crave, or would I miss my royal world? I guessed I would never find out. There was no way I was going to abandon my country and my family. Not even for Ryan.

Especially not for Ryan, a man who'd told me repeatedly that he never wanted to get married or start a family.

Ever.

What kind of future could we possibly have together? He would probably tire of me when the challenge wore off.

Ryan flipped through shows, and I couldn't stop staring at him. He was perfection. His arms were muscular, his profile was distinguished, and he had an adorable grin that could seduce a nun.

A nun, but not a princess.

"What are you in the mood for? There's supposed to be this great documentary about World War Two. You game?"

I was constantly impressed that he binged history documentaries, not reality television. My long-held stereotypes of Americans' viewing habits didn't hold true—at least not when it came to Ryan. "Sure."

The truth was, it didn't matter what we watched, because I simply couldn't focus at all.

My mind was focused on only one thing.

Him.

We had only a couple days left together. A couple days before I flew back home to Santa Cariña.

And less than a month before I got married to Miguel.

How could I ever go through with it? Say "I do" to a man I didn't love now that I had actually *been* in love?

Wait . . .

I was in love.

I'd just admitted it to myself. It wasn't a casual thought. It was the truth.

I loved Ryan.

I needed to tell him now. Even though we could never be anything more than this. Even though we would still say goodbye forever. I needed to tell him this so that for once in my life, I could know what saying those words to someone I adored really felt like.

Before it was too late.

I placed my hand on his thigh, and he immediately put his hand on top of mine. He was so kind, and shockingly, still a perfect gentleman. It baffled me that we had been hanging around each other every day for more than a week, and we still hadn't had sex. When I'd first met him, I thought that he would try to pressure me into having sex with him, but he never had.

He'd never seduced me.

Maybe it was my time to seduce *him*.

But first, I had to tell him something.

"Ry. We need to talk."

He nodded and turned off the television. "Sure. I can't believe we only have two more days left together."

"Me either. But it's not about that. I don't want to talk about that now." The quicksand that was my life, my duties, would swallow me whole before I knew it. But not yet. Not tonight. Tonight, I still had Ryan.

"What do you want to talk about?"

"Sex."

"Look, babe. I'm crazy about you. But I fucking refuse to teach you how to please your new husband or, as he says, 'break you in.'" His eyes narrowed, and a scowl graced his handsome face. "Just the thought of that wimpy, sleazy motherfucker touching you makes me want to slit his throat. Maybe I should have."

Ah. Ryan was jealous. It would almost be cute if he hadn't just threatened Miguel's life.

But this was all my fault. I had gotten myself into this situation. And now there were real feelings involved. How stupid was I to think that I wouldn't fall for Ryan? I'd known the first time I kissed him that my heart was in danger.

"That's not it. Not at all. I don't want to please Miguel."

I took a deep breath. *Here goes nothing.* "I want to lose my virginity to you."

His eyes bulged. "Come again? You're still marrying him, right?"

I nodded my head. "Yes, of course. But it doesn't matter."

He clenched his fists and looked away from me. "Fuck yeah, it matters. I'm not going to be your lover when you're married. You know what I think about cheating and cheaters."

Why wasn't Ryan comprehending what I was saying? "Ryan, listen to me. I'm not married—yet. And Miguel isn't a virgin. Why should I save myself for him? I want to lose my virginity to *you*. Tonight. Now."

His jaw dropped, but he didn't say a word.

Perhaps I needed to be more direct.

I rubbed his cock through his jeans. "Let me suck your cock again."

He pushed my hand away. "What are you talking about? No, not going to happen, Princess."

My heart ached, and my self-esteem plummeted. "Not exactly the response I was hoping for."

He stood and ran his hands through his hair. "What the fuck do you expect me to say? You just want me to let you use me before you run off and marry some other guy? No. I refuse."

I pointed to his face. "*Use* you? You yourself told me that you were a manwhore. That you had slept with hundreds of women. But you won't sleep with me?"

"Exactly. I didn't care about any of them. I've never cared about anyone. But I care about *you!*"

Since the day I met Ryan, he had been the pillar of strength. When I was breaking down, crying, hysterical, he had been calm. But now Ryan's jaw was shaking.

Oh my God. What had I done to him?

This strong man who had never been loved by anyone had finally fallen for someone.

Me.

And now I was going to hurt him.

My body ached like a truck had just hit me.

But it didn't matter. There was no going back. He'd known from day one what he was getting into with me. Hell, he had even admitted that he planned to seduce me and bounce.

Funny how life never worked out the way you wanted it to.

"I want you. I mean it." I pressed my body against his. "I love you, Ryan."

His eyes watered and his mouth opened. I hoped, I prayed, that he would tell me that he loved me too.

But he didn't say a word.

He grabbed me by the waist and kissed me fiercely. He pinned me to the wall as he rubbed my nipples.

"Now, Princess." His voice was husky with lust. "Tell me *now* if you want me to stop so I can get the hell out of here. I can't resist you anymore."

"No, don't stop! I love you, Ryan. Make love to me. Please."

Before I could blink, he picked me up and carried me into his bedroom.

Fear and anticipation twisted inside me. I had held on to this romantic ideal of losing my virginity my entire life. I had pictured candles, a bathtub, champagne, and most importantly, my husband.

None of those things mattered.

My virginity wasn't a prize for me to give away to my husband, or a reflection of my worth.

No. Not at all.

It was an expression of my love for Ryan.

And no matter what, we would always have tonight.

Ryan pulled my tank top over my head and buried his face in my breasts.

His lips grazed my chest, the scruff on his jaw scratching my skin. When his lips finally covered mine, I was already breathless. Though he was definitely in control, he relaxed and allowed me to lead, submitting to the passionate way I wanted to kiss him. The way I wanted him to kiss *me*. Through those kisses, I felt he was telling me what he couldn't say.

That he loved me too.

My body was already so hot and wet, dying to feel him closer to me. Ever since I met him, I had craved his touch, his tongue, his mouth. Everything about him.

And Ryan was a dream come true. He removed my bra and sucked on my nipples. I moaned, and his cock hardened beneath me.

He pulled off my pants in a flash. Within the space of a few seconds, I was completely naked.

He spread my legs wide and devoured my pussy. I ran my hands through his hair, and my back arched as he took me to bliss. As his tongue licked me, I writhed on the bed. In our previous makeout sessions, he had gone so slowly and taken his time.

But now he was moving like he was almost possessed. He gripped my thighs, kissing and sucking on me.

I was so close to coming, but Ryan stopped.

"No, Princess. Not like that. Not tonight. Come here."

Fire coiled in my belly.

"Last chance, babe. Tell me now to stop."

I shook my head. "I want you completely." *Now. Forever.* But I didn't dare say those words out loud.

He grinned, and I melted. He grabbed his wallet and pulled out a condom and tossed his wallet aside. He quickly unbuckled his belt, and his jeans dropped to the floor.

I pulled off his boxer briefs . . . and stared at him standing in front of me, naked.

His body fascinated me. His hard, muscular frame seemed to have been sculpted by Michelangelo himself. And his big, beautiful cock beckoned to me.

Nervousness and desire pulsed through me. My cheeks burned from embarrassment; I was so anxious. Ryan was used to sexually experienced women. How could he possibly enjoy being with me?

"Princess, come here."

He placed his hand behind my neck and gave me a gentle, loving kiss.

I wanted to laugh; I wanted to cry. I wanted him so badly, and I knew deep in my heart that once I went through with this, I would never be the same. Physically, mentally, or emotionally.

Ryan kissed my face and stroked my hair. "I can still stop if you want me to."

"No. Make love to me."

He placed a kiss on my forehead and rolled the condom onto his cock.

Then his hands interlaced with mine as he slowly entered me.

Pleasure spiked with pain shot through me, and I felt a sharp pang. But Ryan didn't allow the pain to last long. He sucked my nipples until I moaned.

I gasped as the pressure grew between my legs. I stretched around him and breathed deeply.

"You okay?"

I nodded but didn't speak. He kissed my neck, my face, my chest as he entered me completely.

"God, you feel so incredible," he gasped.

Our bodies glided together in a rhythm as joy replaced the discomfort. We kissed slowly as he pressed in and out of me.

Then Ryan flipped us over, and I was on his lap as he slowly lowered me down on his cock. At first, the pressure was unbearable, but he kissed me and guided me until my body relaxed.

"You're so beautiful."

His hands clutched my bottom as he pulled me into him. I rubbed against him, and I felt incredible. His mouth took one of my nipples, and I threw my head back.

"That's it, baby. Let go. I got you."

I lost myself in the moment, in him, in us. I was so close. My breath hitched and Ryan took over, guiding my movement, pressing me closer and closer to him until I couldn't hold back anymore. I descended into ecstasy and rode the wave of pleasure with him until we collapsed back down to Earth.

He held me so close and kissed me on the forehead. I never wanted to be apart from him.

He withdrew from me. I looked down beside us— bloodstained sheets. Ryan seemed to notice as well. A proud smile graced his face.

He held me close and kissed me again.

What have I done?

I didn't regret our lovemaking at all. I never would. It was all I wanted and more. But how could I leave now? Tears threatened to consume me.

"Hey, look at me."

I slowly forced myself to make eye contact, blinking back the tears.

"I love you too, Princess."

CHAPTER 24

RYAN

*S*HE LOVED ME? *SHE LOVED ME?*

No one had ever told me that they loved me. Ever. Not my mom. Not my foster parents. No one.

Did she mean it? I doubted it.

Fuck, I loved her too.

But she was promised to another guy. And I had been dumb enough to tell her how I felt too. Now it would be even more painful when she left me.

I went to the bathroom and threw away the condom before quickly returning to her side.

One look at the bloodstained sheets and pride swelled in my chest.

She was mine. She had only *ever* been mine, no one else's.

No one had ever been mine, just mine, and I had never been anyone's.

Why was I being such a pussy? Giselle didn't love Miguel. She loved me.

If I let her fly back home without asking her to stay, I'd regret it for the rest of my life.

And like she said, I didn't live my life with regrets.

She rolled out of the sheets, and I stared at her naked body as she headed into the bathroom. I wanted to wake up with her every day. She came back to bed a few minutes later.

I hugged her. "Babe, can we talk?"

"Of course."

An empty feeling coiled in the pit of my stomach. "I know I don't have much, but I don't want you to go home. Stay here. With me. I'll take care of you."

She turned away from me. "Don't, Ryan. Don't ask me that. You know I can't."

I turned her back to face me. "Why? Why can't you? I can make you happy. You love me, for fuck's sake. I love you. You just lost your virginity to me. Doesn't that mean anything to you?"

"Yes, of course it does. It means everything to me. *You* mean everything to me. But I can't move here. I have a duty to my country. To my subjects. What if I asked you to leave the navy? Walk away from the SEALs forever?"

"That's different. I can't. I'm under a contract."

"No, it's not different—it's the same thing. The exact same thing. You have responsibilities to your country, and so do I."

I knew she was right, although I couldn't help but think there was a way we could make this work.

"Well, what if you just don't marry Miguel? Things could change. I don't always have to be a SEAL." Once I said that I realized how far gone I was with this girl to even consider giving up my career for her . . .

Being a SEAL was all I'd ever had, all I'd ever wanted to be. If I gave that up, I had nothing.

"Ryan, I will marry Miguel. The date is set. We have sent the invitations. The palace has spent so much money on the wedding. I *have* to marry him."

My helplessness turned to rage. "Then why did you tell me you love me? And sleep with me?"

She placed her arms around me, and I rested my head on her chest. "Because I *do* love you. And I am happy that you are the first man I have ever slept with. It was everything I imagined and more. You will always be in my heart, Ryan. It doesn't matter how much I want to be with you . . . I can't."

She was right. We were star-crossed lovers. But no matter how much my head understood, I couldn't explain it to my heart.

CHAPTER 25

GISELLE

$\mathcal{W}$E SPENT OUR FINAL DAY
together making love and taking long
walks on the beach. I never wanted to leave.

Today was the day I would say goodbye to Ryan.
Forever. I felt that we had lived a lifetime in the past
two weeks.

But it was time for my fairy tale to end. I had to go
home.

Ryan drove me to the airport. We hadn't talked much
about our future since the night I'd lost my virginity.
We had both silently accepted the inevitable.

Ryan parked his truck and walked me over to the
check-in counter.

He brushed his hair out of his face. "So, this is goodbye."

"Yes. This is goodbye." I didn't know what else to say. Didn't want to make this harder than it already was. "Ryan, I want you to know something. You're a great man. You have become successful against all odds. You are kind, honorable, and sweet. You took your time with me and were always a gentleman. You taught me so much. I'll never forget you."

He cupped my face one last time. One last kiss. Our lips met, and I savored every second of his touch.

He finally pulled away, a somber look on his face. "You were right."

"About what?"

"I'll never be a prince. Goodbye, Giselle."

And with that, he turned around and walked out of the terminal.

Leaving me alone with my broken heart.

And I knew I would regret saying goodbye to him forever.

CHAPTER 26

RYAN

I GOT INTO MY CAR, BLASTED THE stereo, and headed straight to the beach.

How could I have let her go?

I was a fucking Navy SEAL. I could've fought harder for her. I was a better man than Miguel. Why did he get to marry her instead of me?

Wait—did I want to *marry* her?

The idea of marrying some woman I hadn't even known for a month seemed insane, though some of my buddies married their wives very fast. As SEALs, we never had time to make strong relationships, which was also why our divorce rate was so high. It was hard to build a lasting relationship when we were constantly deployed.

I had told Giselle over and over that I never wanted to get married. Ever. And that I didn't want to have any kids.

But was that still true? I loved playing with my buddies' kids. Maybe it was because I never knew my father. How could I be a good father or husband when I had never had an example of one?

And who had arranged her marriage? *Her* father? King Rémy? Did he really want his daughter to live a life of misery? Did he know what kind of sleazebag Miguel was?

I doubted it.

I picked up my phone. Erik answered on the first ring.

"What's up, bro? Did she leave?"

"Yup."

"You okay?"

"Nope."

"I'm sorry, dude. I remember when Aria left me. I was a mess."

Understatement of the year. I had to drag Erik out of bed to get him to work on time. And he was my commanding officer.

"I remember. But she showed up during basic in your class."

"Yup. Fate has a way of working things out."

"Yeah, well, I doubt Giselle is going to leave her life of luxury to become a Navy SEAL. Or to become a Navy SEAL's wife."

"But you love her, man; I've never seen you pressed like this. Did you try to get her to stay?"

"Yeah, that ship has sailed. I begged her to and she said no. She's a princess. It's not that easy."

"Nothing worth doing ever is."

I paused. No. Love definitely wasn't easy.

But nothing worth having ever was. I had worked so hard to become a SEAL. BUD/S was legit hell. There were so many nights that I had wanted to quit, but I pushed through, knowing the end result would be worth all the pain and misery to get there.

Giselle was mine. I wasn't going to let her go. Not without a fight.

But I had made a mistake by asking her without offering a solution to her problems.

I needed to talk to her father. The king.

Until she walked down the aisle, I still had a chance.

"Hey, can I get some more leave?"

"No, you just got back from Europe."

Fuck. "Please? I'll take your duty for a month."

"When?"

"Now. I have to go stop her wedding."

"Then definitely not. I don't want you to get arrested on foreign soil. I can see the headline now. 'Navy SEAL Gets Arrested Breaking up the Royal Wedding.' No. Didn't you learn anything from me? Remember when I was in the paper with Aria? I was wearing that fucking mermaid tail."

I chuckled. "Yeah, dude. That was fucking hilarious."

"No, it wasn't."

"Then come with me."

"You serious?"

"Deadly."

"Dammit, Ryan." He paused. I never asked Erik for favors. I was the best fucking SEAL in the platoon. I needed him to come through.

"Please, man? This is my only chance. I love her."

He sighed. "Fine. I'll take care of the leave. And you're taking my duty for two months, not one. Also, let's bring Dax along. You know, since he knows the country."

I had the best friends in the universe. They were my family.

It wasn't over between Giselle and me. I was going to get my princess.

CHAPTER 27

GISELLE

I GLANCED AT MYSELF IN THE mirror. My tiara was adorned with jewels, and my dress was hand beaded with a stunning train. My hair had been curled and coifed, and the makeup artist had spent hours giving me the perfect glow.

I looked more beautiful than ever.

But I felt hopeless.

It was my wedding day—it was supposed to be the happiest day of my life, but the girl staring back at me looked miserable.

Breathe. Tears pricked my eyes. *Don't cry. Please don't cry.*

The world would see me as a princess bride, but I saw myself as a fraud. A spineless coward who was about to enter a life of misery and heartache all because I didn't have the guts to stand up to my father, the king, and tell him that I was in love with another man. Not just another man, but a hero, a warrior.

A few hundred years ago, it would've been much simpler. All Ryan would have to do is win a battle and then ask for my hand in marriage. Many countries were founded by warriors. Ryan may think his lineage isn't good enough for a princess, but he was dead wrong.

And Ryan must've forgotten me. I had called him almost daily since I left California. I had planned to beg him to take me back. See if we could find a solution. Even delay the wedding. But once I couldn't get ahold of him, I realized he must have moved on.

It was my fault; I'd told him repeatedly we had no future together. I'd been too scared. Too prideful to make it work.

I would never forgive myself for breaking his heart. And mine.

My aunt and my cousin Lucia walked into the room.

I choked back my tears.

My aunt's eyes brightened. "Giselle, you look beautiful."

A beautiful disaster. I was about to betray my heart—make a vow to a man I didn't love. I couldn't even begin to think about the horror of my wedding night. There was no way I could have sex with Miguel after I had lost my virginity to Ryan. The thought of another man touching me made my skin crawl. My heart still held out for Ryan.

I was so pathetic.

No. I couldn't do this. I was better than just some woman who'd marry for duty. I'd tried and tried, but one last look at my face in the mirror was enough. I couldn't be a bride to anyone but the man I loved.

"Aunt Sophie, I can't go through with this. There's something I need to tell you—"

She placed her finger over my lips. "It's just nerves."

"*No.* You don't understand. I can't do this. I just can't!"

She shook her head. "Now is not the time to get cold feet. It's your wedding day."

Don't remind me. "I know, but I'm not ready."

A smile graced her lips. "No one is ever really ready. You will be happy. I promise."

How could she promise my happiness?

This was it. My last chance to end this charade.

Lucia straightened my veil. "You look gorgeous. Everything will work out."

They both embraced me and then left the room.

I walked out of my dressing chamber, feeling like I was going to throw up. As I headed to the back of the church, I glanced at all the limousines and photographers outside. There was even a horse-drawn carriage waiting to whisk Miguel and me away to our honeymoon suite.

Maybe Miguel would agree to an annulment? There was no way he would want to leave me; he would do what the men in his country were notorious for—long marriages and multiple mistresses.

My father greeted me, his blue eyes blinking back tears. "My princess. You look beautiful. Just like your mother did on our wedding day."

I couldn't hold back the tears any longer. "Papa, I'm so sorry. But I can't go through with this! You don't understand. You see, I—"

He embraced me tight before I could finish my words. "Giselle, I love you. Your groom is an honorable man. All I want is your happiness."

This was it. My last chance. "No, please! I don't want to marry him. I *can't*. I don't love him! Please don't make me do this."

He shook his head. "It's too late; the world has its eyes on you. You must trust me."

My throat burned. He was right. The world was watching—I could've put an end to this at any point up until today. Now it was too late.

I hated myself.

I kissed my father on the cheek and took his arm. We stood behind the massive carved church doors. The notes of the wedding march began, and I knew my fate was sealed. Tears filled my eyes again and I was thankful for my veil.

My father and I began walking down the aisle. Audible gasps filled the church as the crowd stood to greet me. I kept my gaze glued to the carpet, refusing to look at my groom. Maybe when the priest asked if anyone had an objection to this marriage, Ryan would pop up from the back of the pews and whisk me away.

I finally lifted my head and looked around at the standing guests. I scanned the room, but Ryan was nowhere to be found.

Maybe he hadn't really loved me.

No, that wasn't it. That wasn't it at all. I had pushed him away. I had broken his heart. Sleeping with him and then leaving, though he'd begged me to stay. Why on earth would he come to rescue me? I was a monster. Selfish. A pampered princess. I didn't deserve a man like Ryan.

Each step forward was like a dagger in my heart. Instead of appreciating the beautiful music from the string quartet, I was lost within the cacophony in my mind.

I could just reject Miguel at the altar . . .

Yes, that was it! I would say *I don't* instead of *I do*.

I had one last chance to fix this. I was going to take my shot, no matter what it cost me.

We approached the altar, and my resolve grew stronger. I would address the guests and Miguel. Apologize to my country and my family. And then run out the door.

But when I finally looked up—

My mouth flew open, and a flush of adrenaline tingled through my body.

Ryan stood in front of me, a cocky grin on his face, dressed in his black dress uniform with his gold trident pin shining. He had even shaved! I almost didn't recognize him.

Oh my God! What was going on?

My gaze turned to my father, who didn't even look shocked. Did he know about this? Why hadn't he told me?

I then looked back to Ryan, who was standing next to Erik and Dax. They had flown here too?

Where was Miguel?

Was I dreaming?

This was all too overwhelming. My heart raced. Dizziness took hold of my body, but my father held me up.

"Papa, what's going on?"

He spoke in a low whisper, holding my hands in his. "Giselle, Ryan came to me yesterday. Actually . . . he broke into the castle with his friends and slipped by our security."

Ryan had no shame. He could've just called me, but he had to show off. He was full of surprises. I didn't know whether to be pissed off or impressed.

"I was angry—at first. But he told me that he loved you and would do anything for you. He also told me about what Miguel said to you in Paris. I confronted Miguel, and he admitted that he has many girlfriends."

Wow. I was surprised that Miguel had been honest. Maybe he had been dreading this marriage as much as me.

"Ryan's an honorable young man, a warrior. A Navy SEAL. He asked for your hand in marriage, and I gave him my blessing, but only if you will have him. I only want for you to be happy. If you don't want to get married, we can call the wedding off now."

My eyes darted between my father and Ryan. Was this truly happening? My own fairy tale was coming true.

Ryan was at the altar, and my father had given him my hand in marriage.

"But what about Miguel? And our country's military?"

"I talked to Miguel, and he understood. Our countries have always had arranged marriages, but . . . times have changed. I'm the king, so I decided to act like one. As for our military, Ryan and I had a detailed discussion on how we might fix it. And since he will be your husband and a prince, I will consult with him on managing it in the future."

Well, that worked out better than I could have asked for. Miguel would've spent our marriage at the casinos. At least Ryan had expertise to lend to our country.

"I'm so sorry, Papa. I love you so much. I just didn't want to disappoint you. Or endanger our country. You don't know what this means to me. Thank you!" I wrapped my arms around my father's neck, and he kissed me softly on the cheek.

The priest stepped forward. "Who gives this woman to be married to this man?"

My father presented me. "I do."

Ryan offered his hand for my father to shake, but my father embraced him. Then Ryan kissed my hand.

The guests gasped and whispered among themselves. I was well aware that this scandal would be the talk of Santa Cariña for months. And for once, I didn't care what the tabloids thought.

I stared at Ryan through my veil, completely speechless. Ryan pulled me closer, motioning for the priest to wait.

"You look beautiful, Princess. I told you I was never letting you go. But you were forced into accepting one engagement, and I'm not going to make you marry me if you don't want to." Erik handed him a ring, and Ryan knelt before me. "Will you marry me, Princess Giselle Katherine Garabaldi of Santa Cariña?"

I gazed at the ring, a small princess-cut diamond.

It was just perfect.

I choked up. Ryan must've purchased this ring himself, though I was certain my father would have offered him a priceless family heirloom. "Yes. A thousand times yes!"

Our guests erupted in applause.

I wanted to kiss him and jump into his arms, but we had a ceremony to start.

For the rest of the wedding, I was in some sort of haze, incredulous that this had really just happened to me. Where were we going to live? Would he still deploy? But the details did not matter. All that mattered was that we would be together.

Forever.

When the vows began, I choked back tears. But when the priest offered me a script to recite, I pushed it back. Ryan and I had forged our own path—I wanted to be bound to him via my independence too.

"Ryan. You are the most handsome, bravest man I have ever met. God shined down on me the day he placed you in my path. You are the only man I have ever loved, and the only man I *will* ever love. I vow to be faithful, honest, and loyal to you every day of my life."

Ryan wiped away a tear.

"Giselle, meeting you was the best thing that has ever happened to me. My entire life, I've yearned for someone to love, someone who would love me in return, and that someone was you. You are completely out of my league, and I will spend the rest of my life trying to be worthy of your love. I plan to honorably serve your country as well as I serve my own. I never imagined myself as a husband or a father, but now I can't imagine my life any other way."

My heart couldn't take much more. Was this real?

"By the power vested in me, I now pronounce you husband and wife. You may now kiss your bride."

Ryan finally lifted my veil and gave me a slow, sweet kiss. I never thought I'd kiss his lips again. Now I would get to kiss them forever.

"May I now present to you for the first time ever, Prince Ryan Shelton and Princess Giselle Shelton."

He took my hand, and the crowd cheered. My aunt was crying, Lucia was giving me a thumbs-up, and even my father looked pleased.

Ryan led me out of the church and into the horse-drawn carriage. A dozen white doves were released into the sky.

This was the most glorious day.

"Ryan! I love you! I can't believe you came back for me." I gave him a cheeky smile. "But . . . you didn't have to break into the castle. That was a bit over the top, don't you think?"

"Nope. I needed to show your father that he was at risk and that I was worthy of you. You didn't honestly think I'd go down without a fight, did you? I'm a SEAL. You're *mine*. I'm the only man who's ever touched you, and I'm the only man who *will* ever touch you." He cupped my face and gave me a long, sensual kiss. "I fucking love you."

We kissed again, and I lost myself in him. I was the luckiest girl in the world.

"But what are we going to do? Where are we going to live?"

"I made a deal with your father. When I'm training in San Diego, you'll live with me, though he insisted on buying a property in Coronado. When I deploy, you'll return to Santa Cariña. I'll also take all my leave here. And I'll find some retired SEALs to begin working on the military."

"You're the best." My emotions overwhelmed me, and I began to cry. Tears of happiness, shock, joy, and fear all blended together.

Ryan pulled me to him and clutched me to his chest.

"I love you, babe. I'm going to make you so happy. I'll make all your dreams come true."

I looked up at him, his face so handsome. His masculine jawline, strong chin, whiskey-colored eyes. Within his broad chest beat the heart of a warrior. "My dream wouldn't be complete without you in it."

He smirked. "By the way, you were wrong."

Here we go. Been married a minute, and he's already calling me out.

"About what?"

"You said if I kissed you, I wouldn't turn into a prince. Look at me now."

I laughed. "Well, you aren't just a prince. I'm an only child, remember? One day, you will be king."

Thank you for reading The Princess & The SEAL!

I hope you loved Ryan & Giselle.

Catch up with them and meet their friends, Dax &

Mirasol in The Virgin & The Rockstar—A Navy SEAL Rumpelstiltskin Retelling!

Turn the page for an excerpt from
The Virgin & The Rockstar

Or read about Erik & Aria:

***I'm a Navy SEAL, a Triton, a god of the sea.
And she will never be part of my world.***

**Available now: Book 2 in the Heroes Ever
After Series
The Mermaid and The Triton**

**ONE CLICK The Mermaid and The
Triton now!**

XOXO
Alana

$\mathcal{I}$ LOOKED OUT THE WINDOW AS the trained rolled into the station in Bayeux, France. My hand grasped the class of whiskey, and I downed the shot.

I looked over to my wife. "Ready to go, Princess?"

She beamed at me. "Yes. I'm so excited to be back here."

I kissed her on the lips. "Me, too."

I grabbed our luggage, and we exited the train. I glanced down at my designer suitcase—man had my life changed since a year ago.

I was now a prince. Prince Ryan Shelton of Santa

Cariña. It was so surreal to even accept that fact. But the title meant nothing to me. I'd give it all up in a second—as long as I could have still have Giselle.

Giselle pointed to the bench that she had been sitting at when I first saw her.

"Should I sit down? We can reenact how we met."

I shook my head. "Nah. I don't want to beat up anyone today. Let's just check-in."

We had both agreed to go back to the bed-and-breakfast instead of the château.

A camera flashed in my face. But this time, I didn't run after him. Publicity was one of the many things I had to get used to now that I was married to Giselle. But she was worth it.

We arrived at the bed-and-breakfast, and the innkeeper greeted us.

"Bonjour! You two lovebirds! I had no idea you were a princess!"

"Sorry about that."

"Don't apologize! Business has been booming since word got out that you stayed her."

The paparazzo photo the first night we met had been released. Then the guy sued me for assault for knocking the camera out of his hand. I gave him a settlement and had to agree to an exclusive photo shoot.

Since then, I have received extensive media coaching, as well as therapy. I resisted at first but realized that I had to deal with my past. And I was happier than I had ever been in my life, so it was all worth it.

The innkeeper handed me a big key. "I have the same room prepared for you. And let me know if you would like to borrow my husband's motorcycle again."

"We would love to. Thank you."

Giselle ran upstairs, and I chased behind her, carrying our luggage. When we got to the door, I opened it, scooped her up in my arms, and threw her down on the bed.

"Ryan!"

I quickly shut the door.

"You know, that first night, I was so scared. I could never in my life imagine that we would be coming back here a year later. Married!"

"Me either."

My orders had been changed. I had spent the last year in Coronado, training the next generation of SEALs. Giselle purchased a mansion near Dax's and Erik's houses. I really struggled with living in a place like that; I didn't earn it.

But our home was safe and secure. I could walk to work and Giselle would even bring me food when I trained overnight.

Giselle had immersed herself in our community. She organized charity events throughout San Diego. After this vacation, we would go back and stay in Santa Cariña for the summer.

She stroked my hand. "Babe, I've been thinking. I want to start a family."

Whoa. "Now? We've only been married a year. Are you sure?"

"Yes, I'm sure. I mean, I'm supposed to produce an heir."

I rolled my eyes. "Then no. No more doing what you are supposed to do. If you had done that last year, you'd be married to Miguel."

Fucking Miguel. I still hated that motherfucker. A few months after our wedding, he got arrested for raping a woman.

"I know. But it's not just duty. I want a baby. I want to be a mother. I want to have your baby."

A chill washed over me. Was I ready to be a father? How could I be a dad when I never had one?

I closed my eyes and went inward. I loved kids. I loved my wife. I was a good man.

I could do this.

I kissed my wife, cradling her face.

"I love you, Giselle. You will make an amazing mom." I paused. "And I will make a great dad. Let's do this."

She squealed and then wrapped her arms around my neck, kissing me passionately.

"I love you, Ryan. You truly are a prince."

1 THE VIRGIN & THE ROCKSTAR

DAX

I jerked back my head, flinging my blond hair off my face, the sweat dripping down my bare chest. My fingers remained glued to the strings, strumming the final riffs of our rock ballad. Ten thousand rabid fans mouthed the lyrics—the stadium glowed from the synchronized cigarette lighters, the night air pungent with drug fumes. A half naked girl surfed the crowd, minions throwing her on stage, as if they were offering a sacrifice, kneeling at the altar of their rock god—me. What an incredible night. I better fucking enjoy it—because tonight would be my last show, the last time I would make love to this guitar, the last time I would sing our songs. Tonight would be the night my chords would go silent.

But fuck it, tonight wasn't over yet. I was going to live it up. Fuck the finest woman in the audience, get completely wasted, maybe even trash a hotel room. My backstabbing band mates—guys I'd known since we were cub scouts—could go fuck themselves. I'd practiced in my parents' garage with these two-timing sons of bitches since before we reached puberty. We'd broken every barrier in the industry, brought heavy metal music back from obscurity, bridged the gap between rock star and celebrity.

I scanned the crowd, looking for my victim. Usual suspects milled in the crowd—bleached blonde bimbos, marked metal maidens, slutty sorority sisters. But for my last night as a rock star, I wanted someone innocent. Not a virgin, fuck no, I wanted some girl to ride me like a Harley. But I wanted a good girl, a girl who didn't sleep around, a girl who would never dare indulge in her rock star fantasy. A girl who would remember me forever.

What people didn't get about rockstars was that everything was handed to us. Yes men surrounded me, my every whim catered to. I wanted a challenge. For once in my life, I wanted to have to work for something.

My drummer Callan battled the bass drum, and my

throat tightened. This was it. My final note. I plucked the last string, the sound soaring in my ears. A lump grew in my throat, and my eyes watered, but it wasn't from the smoke filled air. It was over. I clutched my beloved guitar, the instrument that had been my lifeline for so many years, and smashed it on the ground. Every bang, every slam, every crack filled me with rage. Chips of wood flew on the stage, strings popped, and I destroyed my prized possession. I glanced back at the audience, my heart pounding in my chest. I gave them a final wave goodbye, flicked off my traitorous bandmates, and exited stage left.

Publicists milled backstage, reporters shoved microphones in my face, and girls screamed when I walked by. Too easy. I wanted something real, a connection. Even though I would never be good for anything more than a one-night stand.

I grabbed a bottle of jack and took a swig; the smooth liquid coated my throat. I was hungry, but wasn't in the mood for the butter-poached lobster waiting in my room backstage. I figured I had a few seconds to make a break for the concessions, before the fans filed out. I dashed out the back door, and entered closest food stand.

Carnal Asada. Kick ass. What a cool fucking name. Mexican food in San Diego was always amazing. I was grateful to have my last show here, one of my favorite cities. I slid to the counter to order some tacos, when something besides food whet my appetite.

Jet-black hair that skimmed her back, huge tits that filled out her t-shirt, jeans that hugged her phat ass. Her plump lips were painted pink, but besides that she didn't seem to have a hint of makeup on. Wow—did this woman have any clue how naturally beautiful she was?

She barely looked up from the register. "What can I get for you?"

"I'll have two *carne asada* tacos and your number."

Her head straightened and her eyes met mine, her lashes rapidly blinking. "Oh my god! You're Dax, aren't you? I'm so sorry I didn't notice you there. What are you doing out here? You'll get mobbed."

People starting exploding out of the concert hall, and she was right, I had to get backstage. "It's cool. Bring me my food to my dressing room." I threw down a twenty-dollar bill and handed her a laminated back stage pass.

She brushed her hand through her hair, and rubbed the back of her neck. I winked at her and gave her my signature head nod. Before she could say a word, I disappeared backstage.

I stalked passed my singer, Trey. Motherfucker, tried to shake my hand. Fuck him. Fuck them all. Guy was a dick, always had been. Long time suffered of LSD, Lead Singer Disease. I was honest to god glad to be free of these fuckers, I just wished I could've left on my own terms.

I opened my dressing room, grateful that the bullshit statement about my departure wouldn't be released until tomorrow. Creative differences my ass. But I refused to be a sob story to the media. I had a plan. Tomorrow I would vanish, and I would make my own path. I was twenty-one, I had my whole life ahead of me.

I peeled off my leather pants and hopped into the shower. The hot water scalded my skin, and I scrubbed the concert off of my chest.

I heard a knock at the door. Great—dinner had arrived. And dessert.

"Dax, uhm it's Marisol, from Carnal Asada? I brought your food. I'll just leave it at the table."

Not so fast sweetheart. "Hey, hold up. I'll be out in a second."

I wrapped a towel around my waist, and opened the bathroom door. "Thanks, babe. Hey, what are you doing tonight?"

Her eyes scanned my body, dropping briefly to my cock but then focusing back on my face. "I have to clean up at the restaurant and then I was going to head home."

I walked over to her, careful to maintain eye contact. "No, you're not. You're coming to Vegas with me."

Her jaw dropped, wide enough for me to imagine my cock in it. "Vegas? You're out of your mind. Don't you have groupies or something?"

I laughed. "Groupies bore the fuck out of me. My bandmates are assholes, everyone in my entourage is paid to tell me how fucking awesome I am. I want a good girl who wants to be bad. Are you game?"

Order Now:

The Virgin & The Rockstar

ABOUT ALANA

 ALANA ALBERTSON IS the former President of RWA's Contemporary Romance, Young Adult, and Chick Lit chapters. She holds a M.Ed. from Harvard and a BA in English from Stanford. She lives in San Diego, California, with her husband, two sons, and five rescue dogs. When she's not saving dogs from high kill shelters through her rescue Pugs N Roses, she can be found watching episodes of Cobra Kai, Younger, or Dallas Cowboys Cheerleaders: Making the Team.

Please join my newsletter to receive a free books!

Newsletter

Website

Email Me

Facebook Group

Inspired by Rumpelstiltskin

Meet Dax! All she has to do to destroy my life is to say my name.

The Maid & The Marine

Inspired by Cinderella

Meet Trace! I will never be her Prince Charming.

The Swan & The Sergeant

Inspired by The Ugly Duckling

Meet Bret! He was a real man—muscles sculpted from carrying weapons, not from practicing pilates.

Rescue Me

Romantic Comedy Series

Doggy Style

Meet Preston! When it comes to doggy style, he's behind you 100%.

Blue Devils

Military Pilots Contemporary Series

Blue Sky

Meet Beckett! I'll never let down my guard for this Devil in a Blue Angel's disguise.

Blue Moon

Meet Sawyer: One Night with this Blue Devil will make you a sinner.

Se7en Deadly SEALs

Navy SEAL Romantic Thriller

Season One:

Conceit, Chronic, Crazed, Carnal, Crave, Consume, Covet

Season One Box Set

Meet Grant! She wants to get wild? I will fulfill her every fantasy.

Season Two:

Smug, Slack, Storm, Seduce, Solicit, Satiate, Spite

Meet Mitch! I'll always be your bad boy.

The Trident Code

Navy SEAL Romantic Suspense Series

Invincible

Meet Pat! I had one chance to put on the cape and be her hero.

Invaluable

Meet Kyle! I'll never win MVP, never get a championship ring, but some heroes don't play games.

Military Contemporary Stand Alones

Badass

Meet Shane! I'm America's cockiest badass.

(co-written with *Linda Barlow*)

Father Figure

Meet Gabriel! Forgive me, Father, for I have sinned.

(Co-written with **Jane Harvey-Berrick**)

ACKNOWLEDGMENTS

I would like to thank my editors for turning this book into what it was meant to be:

Kelli Collins—your razor sharp edits made Ryan shine

Gwen Hayes—clarifying the beats and forcing me to go deeper

Chris—For your amazing line edits.

Lauren Clarke—your coaching has given me such clarity.

To Nicole Blanchard: For listening to my endless rants and encouraging (forcing) me to finish it.

To Kelsey Keeton: for this amazing picture.

To Aria Tan: For creating this gorgeous cover.

To my wonderful husband Roger for loving me and taking care of me while I write.

To my two beautiful sons, Connor and Caleb for your smiles, your laughter, your hugs and kisses.

To all the fans who have been so supportive of my books

Made in the USA
Middletown, DE
01 July 2022